EPHEMERAL CITY

EPHEMERAL CITY

Simon Groth

TINY OWL
WORKSHOP

TINY OWL
WORKSHOP

First published by Tiny Owl Workshop, 2024
Brisbane
tinyowlworkshop.com

Edited by Stacey Clair
Cover and ephemera design by Julia Favaloro
Typeset in Doves Type by Sara Lindberg, Alissa Dinallo Studios

Printed in Australia.

A catalogue record for this book is available from the National Library of Australia

ISBN 978-0-6483746-6-4 (Boxed Edition)
ISBN 978-0-6483746-7-1 (Bound Edition)

Five of these stories have been previously published in earlier versions.

'Blackdrifts' first appeared in *Island, 102* (2005)

'Coda' first appeared in *Syntax, 3* (2002) and later in *Vignette Mini Shots #001* (2007)

'Frangipani' first appeared under the title 'Twelve Years, One Month, and Thirteen Days' in *Meanjin, 65(3)* (2006)

'Gifted' first appeared in *Willow Pattern, a 24-Hour Book*, if:book Australia (2011)

'Heavens' first appeared in *Overland, 175* (2004)

The character of every city is organic and evolving, built over time by generations of stories that are never meant to last, but nevertheless endure. These eight stories and nine pieces of ephemera weave in and out of significant events, told by people from the margins of history, all linked in direct and circuitous ways.

These are stories from my ephemeral city, the place I was born, where I have lived most of my life. A place that is amusing, exhilarating, strange, fantastic, harrowing, heartbreaking, and always intriguing.

—SG

Scan the code below to view the ephemera at your leisure.

Blackdrifts

Floating in nothing, potential space. Warm and secure. Aware only of my existence, no boundaries, no limitations. Smile at the thought that this might be eternity I have entered. It's not frightening. It's the most elegant, relaxing experience I have known. Hang on, catch myself. What else do I know?

> *'...hellnevercraaashpieces*
>
> *...Llllliiiiiiisssssssssssssssssssaaaaaaa?*
>
> *.....maaaaaangledwreckonlysooooo*
>
> *...luckyonlysurvivor*
>
> *...Liiiiiiiiiiiiiiiiiiiiisssa?'*

My name weaves through the mush, in and out of reach. I let it dance around for a moment before shutting it out. For now, no desire, no fear. Duckdive into the calm. Something lurks there, back at the surface of my consciousness. A big bad something, loud and wet. I am aware I can only insulate myself for so long.

◆

I mean sure, from the outside the car's a piece of shit, but under that bonnet it's a different story. She purrs, she growls. She also chews through the petrol, but I'm happy to feed the rusty old EH as much as she can handle. Because when we slip into fifth gear and pelt down an empty highway, my heart wants to fucking explode.

There's four of us inside: the blokes in the front, me and the other chick in the back. In the moment their faces aren't familiar, they could be anyone, but they know me. We've already exchanged electricity, scents, and fluids. That's how it goes.

'What the fuck? Who's that? Oh FUCK, MAN! LOOK OUT!'

I see him (*his golden curls*) and I'm pretty sure he sees me too, even though I'm in the back. Yeah, what the fuck, right? He's standing in the middle of our lane. This bridge is a good kilometre and a half long, fifty metres above the river. How in the flying fuck did he get here? Why would he stand in front of a speeding— and I mean *speeding*—car?

Before I can wrap my head around any of this, we swerve, sharp left. Tyres over wet asphalt. The smell of burning rubber and plastic, leaking petrol, angry speed, and dank sweat.

'No! No! We're going too fast!'

Who was that? What piece of shit would say something so stupid? Not me. As far as I'm concerned, we've barely got going. We plough nose first into the barrier, the bonnet flings up in front of the windscreen and a sickening thump passes through my chest. The scrape of metal on concrete. And we don't stop moving. We never stop moving. We're through the barrier and out the other side. I feel my arse lift off the seat, a pack of ciggies falls across my lap and up the door toward the ceiling. Blood rushes to my head. That creeping, lurching feeling in my guts that I usually welcome. Fast, oh yes everything is fast. Fucking beautiful.

Is this premonition or memory? Am I dead or not yet born?

I'm vaguely aware of pain somewhere, but it seems so far away, out there, nothing to do with me at all. I take deep breaths and hold my position in the void. My mind floats on wave after wave of bubbling warmth.

But the light intrudes, first vague and diffuse, at the edge of my perception. It narrows, brighter, harsher until it's an electric pinpoint. The void closes in. A tunnel exit rushes towards me.

So what? It's a tunnel. Why the fuck should I have to go through it? Just because it's there?

Yes.

No.

It's time.

I emerge, squinting. The light is blinding at first, but resolves into intricate patterns. White knotted tendrils stretch in every direction as far as I can perceive, then further to eternity. I wait for my eyes to adjust and slowly, painfully, eternity flattens then shrinks. I hear the electric hum of machines, punctuated by featureless beeps. A pressed metal plaster ceiling looms. Peeling paint and cobwebs.

'Hi there.' A young female voice outside my field of vision. 'Welcome back.'

Back? I've never been here before. I open my mouth to say so, but nothing happens.

'You're in the hospital. There's been a car—

snap! ceiling coming towards me

—accident. You've been in a coma for thirty-nine days.' Long pause. 'How do you feel?'

I feel like I've been in a coma for thirty-nine days.

There's something surrounding my head, pressing in on my temples. I roll my eyes around as far as they will go, giving myself a headache. I see brushed metal rods, but I can't make out how they are attached to me.

'It's called a halo, the head restraint. It's only temporary. Same with your arm positioning. You have a see-seven ess-see-eye.'

Arm positioning? I have no concept of what that means. My awareness of self dims somewhere around my neck and fades completely around my shoulders. I am told my arms are outstretched, a messianic gesture, maybe a supine crucifix. Along with the halo, I must be a regular daughter of god, delivering salvation to the spiders and the fluoro tubes.

Wait, what the fuck is a see-seven ess-see-eye?

They tell you what has happened at the first opportunity, mix their metaphors, compare your body to an electrical grid, a network of highways. A light goes on. Something happens *out there* and just under the skin the chemistry changes, opening gated channels that speed a message from its source. Up and further away into the crisscrossing expressway of competitive weaving paths, leapfrogging the myelin towards its primary destination. Two lanes merge into four then six as the paths carry ascending messages through the butterfly tracts.

Then stop.

The road is blocked, its lanes torn apart in an orgy of violence. Tissue sheared away from tissue. The messages jumble and drift into oblivion, dispersed into the cerebrospinal fluid, absorbed into the vertebrae, ignored by the ligaments and muscles. The message is lost so absolutely it may as well have never existed.

The sensory cortex, the homunculus with the big-arse lips and bulbous fingertips blinks and scratches his head. Things have been quiet around here lately, but the homunculus doesn't wonder. It is not his role to question, merely to process. He's the middleman, just passing on the message that there are no messages to pass on.

His opposite number, the motor homunculus with the steam-shovel jaw and meat-platter hands is vacantly active. He sends off reconnaissance flares with sickening automatic regularity. It makes no difference to him that his commands go unheeded.

The pair of them squat in the cortex like Dumb and Dumber waiting for Godot.

And between them, darkness flows in drifts of flat, low nothingness.

◆

He breezed in and hovered over me. The sweet cool aroma of cologne drifted after him, filling the air with goodwill. His blonde hair (*golden curls*) was clipped and cropped against his skull. Without a word he made me feel like I was the only person that mattered to him. When he smiled, his ivory keyboard was crisp and bright.

'Good morning, Lisa. We've met plenty of times before, but you probably don't remember.'

Mate, I was in a void, a place that wasn't a place at all, monks chanting, book of the dead shit. I was nowhere near here. I've only just arrived in this world.

'I'm Brad, by the way.'

Seriously? Brad? It seemed the only thing about him that wasn't perfect.

'Hello.' My voice was croaky and stilted. Disabled.

Brad consulted the chart in his hands for a moment. 'We'll be getting you out of this halo soon enough. Then you'll find out what a sadistic bunch we physios really are!' and he threw his head back and snorted. I had no idea what he found so funny about sadism—I guess whatever floats your boat, man—but he had an infectious laugh and I wheezed along anyway.

❧

A hot summer, days ablaze in golden brown. I know he is here as we pull up in the parking lot. His cassette deck cranks the sounds of Talking Heads (*life during wartime*), Midnight Oil (*back on the borderline*), and Joy Division (*love will tear us apart*). His car, an immaculate EH sedan, parked on an angle to show off its gleaming panels, the chrome strip running up the side like a sexy split skirt.

The beach is ahead, a small patch of coarse, dark sand cleared between the mangroves. Roots rise from the mud either side like beds of nails. The water beyond is not the ocean, no cool crested waves rolling in. This is the river, brown like weak tea. The only waves are from the boats that pass by in the middle.

Though I've already seen his car, a flush of relief swells when I spot him swimming. Every time we come here I hope to see him, but usually I'm disappointed. Not today. The boy with the golden curls wears his hair long like a surfer. He moves with effortless grace, as smooth in the water as he is on the bank. He smiles at us and I smile back.

I take my shoes off and curl my toes into the sand, grit under my toenails. Mum rubs coconut oil onto my back so that I'll get nicely tanned, like the boy with the golden curls. But it never works. I'm a burner, always have been.

I enter the water braced against the cold, but it takes my breath anyway. I splash about to speed up my acclimatisation. I edge closer to where the boy is treading. I call out to him (*hey*) ask him about his car, but he ignores me, swims out further. I try to follow, but the water turns black. Murky drifts of void open under my feet. Something about that black water scares me. I mean, anything could be hiding there and I'm sure one time I felt something slither at my feet. But my fear comes from something more fundamental, the thought that I might venture too far and never find my way back again. It's a thought that, once I've acknowledged it, grips me harder until I whimper and splash back to the bank. My brother laughs and calls me a wuss, which tells you all you need know about him. But the boy with golden curls loves the black. He loves the void. That's where he lives. He duckdives into it: his head goes under, his feet appear for a second before they too sink into the black. I count. I count to a hundred and twelve, tears rolling down my fat cheeks and I am sure he's dead, that the darkness itself has taken him from me forever. When his head pops up again, jack-in-the-box, he's downstream towards the next reach, a long way from where he went under. Hair clings to his cheeks in ringlets.

You never resurface in the same place you sank.

◆

I never told anyone about the void, my void I mean, that warm cosy cocoon. I didn't feel right to tell the people helping me recover that I might actually have preferred the blackdrifts of coma. I clung to the memory of it. I feared that each passing day I remained exposed out here, this new reality would eat away at me, hollowing me out until I lost the only part of my existence that made any sense.

Brad would come and fuss over me. Sometimes, he flipped me over so I could see something other than ceiling (*white panels, naturally*), even if it was only the dust and hair on the vinyl floors (*flecks of grey, television static*). The bed was capable of rotating a full hundred and eighty degrees. Facing down meant I would hang, strapped in, suspended. Ancient torture masquerading as traction.

When he wasn't there I waited for him. When he was there I absorbed him, breathing in deeply, filling myself with the sense of him.

'How's it hanging?'

Hilarious, Brad. I decided to be honest for a while and let him in on my stupid daydream fantasies.

'I'd rather be sitting by a pool in Mallorca smoking a fresh ciggie, wearing a G-string bikini that shows off my freshly liposucked thighs.'

'Mind if I join you there?'

Did he read my fucking mind?

'It would hardly be a party without you.'

Well done, Lisa. Cool as a cucumber, babe.

'Have you been?' he said.

'Mallorca? Get fucked! Can't drive there.'

'Never been overseas at all? No booze cruises with mates?'

'I don't go places, I look at them on maps. Besides, the guys I used to hang out with were deadheads. Complete morons. You're not going to find them on a fucking cruise, even one with booze.'

'I'd hate to see what you say about people you don't like. Remind me to stay on your good side.'

'Nah, you're nothing like them.' I'm nothing like I was. 'Those guys couldn't scratch their own arses.'

'So Spanish islands are your go-to fantasy?'

'I dunno. Paris would be alright.'

Brad smiled. 'Oh, you'd love Paris. Everyone does. The streets around the Sacre Coeur are like a movie set. Artists set up their easels on the street and paint the passers-by. They'd clamber over each other to paint you, gushing over such *yeux exquis.*'

I had enough high school French under my belt to recognise the phrase: 'exquisite eyes'. Lucky the car wreck didn't take those away. Lucky Brad the physio was not a legs man.

'For fuck's sake, Romeo. You don't have to be such a tryhard!'

When I climb into that back seat, I know exactly what I'm doing. I know what I want. It's dark, either late or early depending on your perspective. The car's humming and four empty lanes await. We pause only to toss a handful of coins into the toll basket, then we climb that concrete arch, ascending to heaven. When they opened this bridge, people queued up to jump off it. Then they put up a barrier, so now you can't see the view so well. We roar to the top of the bridge, the EH gives us everything she can cope with. I want nothing less than to lift off, sail this bitch into the sky and drift into the atmosphere. Somewhere below would be the old beach where I used to swim before this bridge was built. Maybe once we hit heaven I could look for the boy with the golden curls. He exists up there in the darkness. Heaven is his stomping ground.

'Keep your foot on that fucking pedal!' I scream. My voice is unrecognisable, shrill and urgent. My limbs tingle. I am loose and warm, heat radiating from between my thighs.

◆

Still in bed. Yet to meet the wheelchair, but soon to be out of the halo, no longer converting heathens on the ceiling and floor. Brad's face appeared before me, suspended in space.

'It's okay. Go ahead,' he said. 'How does it feel?'

I could move my arms. I could feel a little in my fingertips. This was all new. Lisa McAuley was no longer a floating head. The dull amorphous pain I had become so accustomed to had sharpened into something hard and heavy. I reached my new arm out, my new fingertips grazed his cheek.

'When was the last time you shaved?'

He smiled. 'A couple of days ago. Blonde stubble is not so noticeable from a distance.'

His lips were red and wet. He looked at me with eyes from far away, his pupils a gateway to the deepest part of the void. I moved my hand from cheek to chin, from chin to lips. He cleared his throat and withdrew from the bed.

There was something real there.

Real discomfort.

More than that, it was the old swagger, the way I used to be.

There is no before, only the void and the boy with the golden curls. Remember him?

What, he's all grown up into Brad the godlike physio?

Ask him what kind of car he drives.

✦

The second I woke up I was fussing. With the halo off and my arms free, I was ready to be transferred to another ward. I sat upright in a wheelchair—crappy, standard issue with padded armrests would you believe—near the door. Beyond that door was something new, terrifying and exhilarating.

'Is my hair right?' I asked the nurse who changed my catheter bag.

'Absolutely, Lisa. You look gorgeous. Who's the bloke?'

I smiled. I knew my hair was flat on the back and too poufy in the front. Nurses will lie to you, but they'll do it so sweetly that you don't care.

'I don't know what you're talking about.'

'Oh *sure*, darling.'

What Brad knew of me was shielded behind a metal frame. He saw me as someone imprisoned, strapped to a table like I was awaiting a lethal injection. It was an unfair test of this new life. This was now the real Lisa McAuley, crappy wheelchair and all.

For the first time since I was twelve I longed for cosmetics. I experimented with touching my own face, checking the firmness of my skin, but my fingers stayed slightly curled like a chimpanzee's. I couldn't straighten them. The best I could manage was towing fingertips across my cheek so they rolled open and dragged my lower eyelid and the corner of my mouth down. The mirror in the corridor opposite reflected what appeared to be someone with a stroke rather than a spinal cord injury.

I closed my eyes and shook my head. As I did, I sensed someone passing by behind me.

'Good morning, Candy! How's my little supermodel this morning?'

'Hi Brad.' She giggled like a fucking schoolgirl.

I peered around the pillows. Hey! He walked right past without as much as a basic greeting. Made a beeline straight for the fourteen-year-old fresh from a horse-riding accident. Horse riding for fuck's sake! She scored herself a C3-4 fracture, much worse than mine. There was little doubt even in my longest days in the halo that I would get back arm movement, hopefully thumbs too. Poor old Candy-girl had nothing to look forward to but painting landscapes with a brush jammed between her teeth.

'Hey Brad! Over here!' I called out.

'Well hell!' he said over his shoulder. 'Look at you!'

'Yeah, look at me.'

'Well done, Lisa. I'm going to spend some time with Candy today, but I'll catch up with you on the new ward. Maybe tomorrow, huh?'

'What the fuck? I'm out of the halo!'

'Yeah, I see that. It's fantastic.' short and clipped.

Was he being terse? 'We'll finally get around to doing some proper work together once you're transferred, but today it's all about Candy.'

Another fucking giggle.

'Sure,' I muttered, narrowing my eyes at them. 'Just one question before you go do your thing: what car do you drive?'

'Sorry?'

'What kind of car do you drive?'

'Why do you want to know that?'

'I just want to know. What difference does it make why?'

'It seems like a strange question to ask out of the blue.'

'I'm pretty strange. Humour me.'

He took a step backwards and shrugged his shoulders.

'A Volvo,' he said eventually.

I couldn't help but laugh. 'Have you got one of those little hats to go with it?'

'I chose it for safety, not for looks.'

My smile dropped. Brad wasn't chasing sexy. He wanted the safe bet. He wanted to walk away unharmed if it all turned to shit.

Are we still talking about cars?

Pull it together, Lisa.

'I reckon people who prioritise safety should just learn how to be better drivers.'

She's in shock.

Shock, shock. Horror, horror.

It's a natural reaction. She'll come around soon.

You hear about these freaks all the time. Read about them in the papers. Sometimes the current affairs shows will do a piece on them.

Fetishists.

I've heard it all: people who get off on watching other people sleep, women who go only for men with hairy shoulders. Any number of feet, necks, elbows. I heard of this one dude who liked to lick women's teeth. That's it, no sex or anything. Just wanted to lick those pearly whites. Then there are the ones who go for amputees, white canes, wheelchairs.

A hospital is a smorgasbord of pain, misery and suffering for people who need to feel needed. Just as sure as it attracts multi-resistant bugs, it attracts the fetishists. Moths to a fucking flame.

You know what?

Leave me alone.

You need to get your shit together, Lisa. Make a decision.

About what?

Are you going to make something of this new life or crawl back into the void?

Don't tempt me.

What's it going to be?

◆

Time does funny things in the crumpled cabin of a rusted, roaring EH as it breaks through and takes flight. Gravity shifts up, down, forward, and back as we roll through the night sky. With the bonnet up, I can't see straight ahead, but from my window, I see nothing but stars. For one, glorious, beautiful moment, I reach the place I've always dreamt of. In the distance, moonlight illuminates streaks of cloud, a staircase of light ascending to—

Where?

The car is drawn higher and higher, rising on thermals. I take a sharp breath in the thinning air. A face, a familiar face, emerges from behind the clouds. Even from this distance I see his long hair catching, absorbing cool moonlight, generating its own waves of calm. His eyes—

yeux exquis

—beckon. One by one my silent travelling companions open their doors and drift into the air after him. I pull the seat belt fast across my lap.

'Don't you even care about your own fucking car?' I cry at them.

My head fogs as I gradually become aware of pain. Somewhere down below, the river slithers, writhes. I jam my feet against the front seat bolts and grab the shit-bar above the window. The car's nose lowers; I watch the dark horizon rise and rise as my once rocketing capsule loses momentum and falls to earth. A slick of lunar reflection separates into individual waves, ripples, eddies, and currents.

I am acutely aware of what is happening. The car is burning oil. The smell of the upholstery, the loose cigarettes rolling around, the fresh plastic, the sweat and scum on the cream coloured steering wheel, the dust and grit on the mat at my feet, the wet nose marks of some unknown dog at the bottom of the window.

Then impact.

Snap.

Water as hard as concrete.

I disappear into the black, no longer afraid. The car is drawn into dangerous undercurrents, sucked deeper, but I'm no longer there. A vast expanse of nothingness opens before me. It reaches out and embraces me, fills me relief and contentment. I don't even care about the boy with the golden curls any more. Who needs a slut like that around anyway?

Sixpence

The walk doesn't worry the boys, they don't wear shoes anyway, except to church on Sunday. Mum told us ladies don't go barefoot and ever since I always wear my shoes and Alice never wears hers. Only now one of my shoes has a hole in it. Alice offered to swap, but Mum wouldn't let us. Georgie showed me how to patch it up by putting a piece of thick card inside, but it keeps coming loose and I can feel the gravel.

'Keep up, you two!'

'We're comin' Georgie! Keep ya pants on!'

My brother squints at Alice. 'What are you up to?'

'Nothin'. Boo thought she saw a ha'penny on the ground.'

Georgie to me, 'Well, didja?'

I look down at my shoes when I talk to him. His eyes always look angry. 'Nah. Think it was a pebble.'

'Well stop mumblin' and move. We hafta be at the theatre by eleven. That's when they're drawing!'

We start off again, two by two like we usually do. Georgie and Rose up front, then Laurie and Francis, then Alice and me at the back.

I thought we were on our way to the lottery, but Georgie's talking about a drawing. I don't know what kind of drawing it is. I reckon it should be a picture of a big house with big trees and a garden full of flowers and honeybees with a big round pond in the middle and stuff. I'd like to see a drawing like that.

I want to ask Alice about it, but I can't without the others hearing me and I know they'll make me feel like a dill. When they laugh or sometimes when they go crook at me all I want to do is crawl into a safe place just me and Alice. I can rely on her; she sticks up for me. Well, all she can really do is put on a show, use her smarts and her mouth, but she's still my best defence.

She stops suddenly and my arm is pulled back. We'd drifted towards the road and Alice stopped us right in front of a trough. A step further and she would have barked her shin.

'Whydja stop?'

'There's horses. And it felt like you weren't payin' attention, Boo.'

Alice notices stuff like that. She just kind of feels it when she's holding onto my arm. I guess it's just what happens when you can't see nothing. Your eyes don't get in the way of your feeling. She's the same with sounds and smells and stuff: when the milkman's big Clydesdales clop past our road, when the outhouse needs changing, when the stove loses heat and needs more wood, when potatoes are full of grubs. This is the kind of stuff she notices, usually ages before anyone else. She gets around the house without any help, slides her hands along the walls, sometimes leaving streaks of dirt or grease behind her, but when we're out and about Alice holds onto my elbow.

She's blind as a bat and I don't say boo. That's why we've got to stick together, even though she's a whole year and twelve days older than me. It's always me who leads her around but she's the one who tells me where to go. I'm always describing stuff for her and she tells me what's going on.

Sometimes I close my eyes so I can see what things are like for Alice, but it's hard. I can only close my eyes for a few seconds before they start fluttering back open again, especially when I'm moving around.

'Hey Laurie, look at this! It's the blind leading the blind!' Francis is talking to my other brother. They're both older than us.

'What are ya talkin' about?' says Alice.

'You two are getting more like each other every day.'
That's Laurie.

'Whaddaya doin', Boo?' Alice asks me.

'She's got her eyes closed, Bats. She wants to be more like you! Reckon you should aim higher, Boo!'

I keep my eyes closed. I hate seeing people laughing at me.

'What's the matter, Boo?' Alice whispers into my ear. 'If you get picked today, I'll help ya out.'

'Hey, what's the matter, Boo?' says Francis. He sounds like he's singing.

'You leave her alone! If ya wanna pick on someone, pick on me!'

'Pick on you, huh?' My eyes flutter open in time to see Francis give Laurie a nod.

'Where are ya? Ya big creeps! I know you're there!' Alice waves her arms around in a rage.

Francis pushes her first, then Laurie joins in. They look like magpies circling, nipping at her from all sides.

'Hey stop it! I'm a helpless blind girl!'

'That doesn't work with us, Alice!'

'Yeah, you're about as helpless as a... Hey Georgie, what's somethin' that's not helpless?'

'Start walkin' and stop yappin' or I'll tell Mum and Dad on the lot of you!' Georgie bawls back. In silence, we fall back into line.

Soon, Alice squeezes my hand. I know what she's telling me. I squeeze back and together we speed up, drawing closer right up behind our middle brothers. When we look about the right distance I squeeze Alice's hand again.

She kicks her foot up high and connects with Laurie's bum. Alice doesn't need shoes to kick hard.

'Ow! Ya little runt!' Laurie spins around, his eyes wild. I hold onto Alice's hand as tight as I can and run towards the pub on the corner. 'Come here so I can kick your brains out!' Laurie screams as Francis breaks from the line and chases us.

'Oi! Get back here you lot!' Georgie shakes his fist in the air like an old man.

❧

He smiles at us from the top step of the pub. As we get closer, I realise he's smiling only at Alice. He barely notices me. His trousers and coat are tatty and his hat is squashed this way and that. He holds a Gladstone bag with both hands in front of him.

'Hello darlin'!' he says.

'Hello mister,' says Alice, like she knew he was there. She does that sometimes. She reckons she can hear people and sometimes smell them when they're close by.

'You're a pretty little thing, aren't you? But I tell you what would make you even prettier!' He smiles again and I notice how yellow his teeth are. He sets his port down on the step in front of him, unclips the top, and rummages inside.

'Who's this?' I whisper into Alice's ear.

'I dunno.'

The others catch up as the bloke pulls a long strip of blue ribbon from the bag. Laurie and Francis watch in silence, their mouths open. Trying to catch flies, as Dad says. Georgie shoots a look at Rose, who shrugs in reply.

'Here.' The bloke holds the ribbon out to us. It dangles from his fingers like a dead snake. 'Wear this and you're sure to stand out from the crowd.'

Georgie steps forward. 'Sorry, sir,' he says. 'We can't accept that. Mum says we shouldn't accept a present from somebody we don't know.'

'Georgie! He's givin' it to *me*!' Alice cries. She doesn't even know what it is.

'Your Mum's a wise lady, son. But all I'm offering is a ribbon for your little sister to put in her hair.'

'Yeah!' says Alice.

Georgie rubs his chin like he's got whiskers there. He checks again with Rose who nods. Eventually he says, 'Alright, I guess if it's just a ribbon. You can take it, Bats.'

'Thanks, mister!'

'Are you off to the pictures, little one?' says the bloke.

'Nah, to the lottery,' Alice replies.

'The lottery?' He tips his hat back and scratches his head. 'You watch yourselves down there.'

Rose ties the ribbon into a neat bow in Alice's hair.

'How's it look, Boo?'

'It's blue.'

'Blue, huh?'

I wonder sometimes what she imagines when we talk about colour. Alice reaches up and feels the ribbon, smiling as she does. It's tied to a tuft of hair sticking straight up from her head. She twirls the hair around her finger like she does to my hair when we go to bed at night.

'Come on.' Georgie takes my hand on one side and Alice's on the other, walking between us. 'I gotta keep a close watch on you two from now on.'

'Thanks again, sir!' Alice yells back over her shoulder.

'You give those jokers at the lottery hell!' he calls back. 'A hundred quid I was supposed to get!'

'What does that mean?' I ask Georgie.

'From an old drunk like that? Prob'ly nothin'. They should lock 'em up, people like him.'

After a while, I look back up at him. 'Georgie, why do they lock people up?'

'Aw, you know. If they're bad.'

Bad? Right away I think of Mrs Langtry and her little talk with Mum the other day. What has Alice done that's so bad?

❧

I wasn't supposed to be inside. Mum always shoos us out when Mrs Langtry visits. I only went back to get my dolly, but when I heard them talking about Alice I stopped next to our bed in the sleepout.

Mum put the tray with bikkies and tea on the table. I couldn't believe she was giving away our last bikkies. They sat back in their chairs and sipped their tea without saying anything.

After a long time, Mrs Langtry said, 'Elizabeth, I wouldn't say this unless there had been some serious disquiet from the parish ladies.'

'Disquiet?'

'They...we've been concerned that Alice should receive the best care possible. These are hard times and it is difficult to make ends meet, especially with six children. But for a child like Alice to be wandering the streets by day...'

'Mrs Langtry, Alice is not a silly girl. And I don't think a bit of mischief means she should be locked up!'

'Locked up? Good Lord, you make it sound so dramatic! But to some extent you're right; this mischief is just what I'm talking about. It indicates a problem. An active mind being held back. She's at the age where she recognises how different she is.'

'But she's got little Betty to help her. The pair of them are never apart. Alice is good for Betty too, she's such a shy little thing. Helps her come out of her shell.'

'It's wonderful that Alice has some help. But that doesn't change the fact that she is a little blind girl.'

'She's got plenty of confidence.'

'And that confidence only leads to trouble. Look,' Mrs Langtry set her tea down and crossed her legs, 'she has been caught playing in some horrid back streets, shooed out of shops on the terrace and she's even made tomfoolery with older boys near the tavern. These are places a little girl like Alice should never be. People are talking; they're concerned. Father Logan himself has asked me to make this visit to you. Alice's place is in an environment where she can be cared for the way she needs to be. And if the family cannot provide that, then we have a Christian duty to see that alternative arrangements are made.'

'All this talk of "care"! She's blind, not sick.'

'But don't you see? That's precisely my point.'

They both say nothing for a while, hardly moving. I was trying to work out what they were talking about. Were they going to send Alice to gaol or something?

'How is Jack getting along?'

'Better. He's laying pipes for the new town water. They're long days, and he is not used to using his hands like that, but thank God he has some work again. People just aren't buying books anymore, there's no money for it.'

Suddenly Mrs Langtry stood. 'Elizabeth, I must be on my way. You send Jack the warmest regards from myself and Mr Langtry. Remember, you don't have to look after Alice alone. There are ladies in the parish who *will* help.'

Mum rubbed her forehead. 'Thank you, Mrs Langtry.'

'Thank *you*, Elizabeth, for the lovely tea. Now think about it. I'll see you on Sunday.'

◆

'What's it like?' Alice whispers into my ear.

'There's stairs out the front here and lots of people.'

'I can hear the people. What are they doin'?'

'Dunno. Waitin' to get inside I think. There's a couple of motor cars stopped out front.'

'Can we get up close to 'em?'

'I think so.'

'Show me.'

I take Alice over to the car and place her hand on its shiny black metal. We don't get up close to an automobile much. Usually they're surrounded by older boys and men. Alice puts her palm down flat on the bonnet and runs it slowly across.

'Nice,' she says quietly.

'It's shiny like a mirror. I can see our 'flections in there.'

'Come on!' Georgie bustles us into the theatre. 'Now remember what I said, Boo. They reckon the lottery people really go for littlies, so you gotta be ready.'

'Hey what about me?' says Alice. 'I'm little!'

'Boo's littler. And besides you wouldn't see the ball to get it out of the barrel, they can't pick you!'

'Why not? I could use four shillings and sixpence. Hey Boo, think of all the humbugs we could eat for four and a half bob!'

'You wouldn't get all of it. We'd each of us get threepence each and that's it.'

'Why are they givin' money out anyway?'

'That's what the lottery is all about. They call it the Golden Casket. It's like they got all this money and they have to give it out to people who need it. But b'cause there's so many people who need it they get them to choose numbers so it's all fair. And they gotta choose those numbers somehow, so they pay kids like us to do it for them.'

'Why kids?'

'I dunno.'

My brother Francis speaks up. 'If we get threepence each, what happens with the other three shillings?'

'It's for Mum and Dad. Now when we get inside we're gonna split up.'

'Split up?' Alice screws her nose up.

'Yeah, we're all gonna sit in separate spots.'

'Why?'

Georgie sighs. 'Because they'll only ever pick one of us if we all sit together. Now remember, you gotta be ready if they pick you, Boo.'

I feel like my tummy's all twisted and creeping up to my throat. 'What do I do?'

'First thing's first. You gotta smile. Big smile, show me.'

I show my teeth.

'What the hell's that?'

'Boo you gotta smile like this!' says Alice. She's lost track of where I'm standing and grins madly at some bloke standing near us. He frowns but tilts his hat towards her anyways.

'Both of you look like you're in pain!' says Rose, hands on her hips. 'Just a nice big smile, Boo, you know like those posters outside the Plaza.'

'Uh huh.'

'Now act natural,' Georgie keeps going, 'don't run, just walk calmly. The bloke up the front will tell you what to do. And don't mumble, you gotta speak clear and loud, but don't shout.'

'Boo doesn't know how to shout!'

'Yeah thanks, Rosie. Now Boo, don't worry about Bats. She'll be fine, we'll keep an eye on her. So long as she shuts up for half a minute, everything will be fine.'

)

'Pick me, pick me, pick me!'

'Alice, shut up!' I hiss out the side of my mouth.

'How about…the little girl with the bow in her hair!'

'Oh shoot! He's lookin' at you, Bats!'

'Such a pretty bow, why dontcha come on up here and pick a number out for us!'

Alice shifts in her seat and smiles. I know that smile.

The host who introduced himself as 'Gordon Spoon' has a thin moustache and his hair is slicked back with a line around where his hat would usually sit. He comes down from the stage and approaches us, his big straight teeth gleaming.

A step closer and the smile is gone. He stops dead and pulls at his collar. They're all the same. They start out thinking Alice is normal, then when they get closer they notice her eyes, all screwy and bloodshot.

'Oh…*hel-lo lit-tle girl! CAN YOU PICK A NUMBER?*

'Course I can Mister Spoon. I'm blind, not deaf and dumb.'

A few chuckles from the people around us. I sink down in my seat and wait for this to be over.

'Only thing is,' says Alice, 'I'll need to take my sister up there with me.'

He looks at me. 'You're her sister?'

'I'm Betty. She's Alice.' I try smiling like Georgie said.

'I can't hear you, darling.'

'I'm Betty. She's Alice.'

'Stop talkin' into ya chest, Boo,' Alice mutters.

With his voice lower, Gordon Spoon says to me: 'Will she be...alright?'

'Of course I'll be right,' Alice says in that singsong way she does, 'Boo here is my eyes.'

'Um...,' he stares at us then smiles big and wide again, 'well give 'em a hand, folks.'

The carpet feels hot through the hole in my shoe. Alice holds my elbow and pushes me in front of her.

At first the place is real quiet, people talking in low voices. I hear somebody on one side say, '...shouldn't be allowed...' and on the other side, 'What's wrong with her?'

Alice would hear more of it than me. She's pretty sharp and she always knows when people are talking about her. Usually she'll then do something stupid like grope at my face or something. Sometimes she asks me to tell her where they are so she can 'stare' at them. But today she just follows me to the stage.

'Tell me about it again, Boo.'

'It looks *fancy*.'

'Fancy doesn't tell me anything! Gimme detail!'

I look up. 'There's a real big chandelier,' I say, 'and so beautiful like there's *hundreds* of little diamonds hangin' together and up real high. Remember Mum's necklace? The one she sold to Mister Blamey? It's like that only a hundred times bigger.'

'Hundred times? Holy Dooley! How did they get it up there? All those diamonds?'

'I dunno. Must have big ladders and stuff.'

'You know what? I'm going to have a big, fat diamond necklace just like that chandelier after this and everyone will look at it and know I'm rich. I'll wear it all the time, even in bed, except when you wanna borrow it.'

'It's huge, Bats. You'll be draggin' it behind you, not wearin' it.'

We climb the stairs to the stage, clomping on the rough wooden boards. Ahead of us, Gordon Spoon turns the barrel of numbers, staring out at the audience with a toothy grin, bursting with scary excitement.

'Boo?'

'Yeah?'

'Somethin' doesn't sound right. What do you see?'

'He's turning the barrel. It's like a big round cage with a handle at the side. Inside are all these little balls, little marbles.'

'So when he stops, I pick a marble out, right?'

'I think so.'

'Right, so what I'm tellin' ya is that the marbles sound funny.'

'Stop foolin' around, Bats. We'll get into trouble.'

'Hey, what's that?'

'What's what?'

'Those footsteps over there.'

'I dunno, there's a curtain. Somebody must be behind it.'

'A curtain, huh?' She reaches out and paws at it. 'Ooh it's velvet!'

'Bats, stop doin' that!'

We reach the barrel. Gordon Spoon stops turning the handle and turns his grin to us.

'Okay girls, now don't be frightened. When I say so, you come over here and pick a ball out, okay?'

'Mister Spoon?'

'Yes, dear?' he looks at me, even though he is talking to Alice.

'There's somebody sneakin' around back there, I hear footsteps.'

The man pulls at his shirt collar again. 'Pay no attention to the man behind the curtain,' he says, waving a hand. 'That's the government official.' He steps out to the front of the stage again and speaks to the crowd.

'I'm not jokin' Boo,' Alice says. 'There's somethin' really fishy goin' on here. I reckon they've got cats eyes and clunkers in there.'

Cats eyes are the regular marbles we always play with. There's a kid lives down the hill from us who's got a big clunker, heavy as anything. One time me and Alice were playing near the shop and this kid comes up with his clunker and plays for keepsies. Clean stole all our marbles out from under our noses. Alice faked cryin' and yelled that he stole marbles off a blind girl. That brought out Laurie and Francis who beat the kid up for us. We got our cats eyes back.

'So what if they got some clunkers in there?'

'They're heavier Boo. They'd always sink to the bottom.'

'So?'

'They're cheatin'. They're makin' sure that some numbers always come up! They're havin' the wood on us!'

'This ain't funny.'

'I swear! I reckon it's a lurk.'

'Yeah well we still get our sixpence.'

'But what about all them other suckers who paid for a ticket? They're gettin' robbed!'

'Come over girls! Come and pick out a number!'

I look out into the room, a wall of faces stare back at us. I pick out Georgie and I'm surprised to see he doesn't look angry. Francis and Laurie are cheering and clapping. Rose shakes her head slowly, grinning. I guess that should make me feel better, but I can't shake off the feeling of all the other people watching my every move. I break out in a sweat, my mouth dirt dry. My heart hammers at my chest. When I spot Mrs Langtry looking grim at the back of the hall, my knees weaken. Alice notices my hand shaking in hers.

'What's the matter?'

'Nothin'.'

She doesn't believe me, but she doesn't keep on it.

'Come on,' she says gently.

At the barrel, Alice plunges her hand right to the bottom and roots around in there.

'Just one number dear! We've five more kids after you!' Gordon Spoon winks at the crowd and they laugh.

Alice ignores him and keeps swirling her hand around the bottom.

'What are ya doin'?' I whisper.

'I'm lookin' for the clunkers.'

'Everyone is looking at us. Just take one so's we can get outta here.'

Gordon Spoon looks annoyed and mutters to me: 'Maybe you should help her.'

'There's no proper clunkers. The heavy and light ones must all be the same size.'

'You're takin' forever!'

I look back out. None of my brothers is smiling anymore, nor is Rose. I'm too scared to look for Mrs Langtry.

I don't care about the marbles or our sixpence anymore. I try to pull Alice away by her hand.

'Alice! Let's go!'

Gordon Spoon leans down and talks through his teeth. 'Listen you little rats, I don't know what you're up to, but you're holding everything up. Now pick a bloody number and bugger off!'

Alice replies in her loudest voice, which easily fills the whole room. 'Mister Spoon, I'm only tryin' to get to those heavier marbles at the bottom. And I'm no rat! I'm the daughter of Jack and Elizabeth Marshall.'

I think what happens next is what they call a gasp. Murmuring and shifting in seats. Gordon Spoon looks out to the audience and laughs, but no one laughs with him. The murmurs get louder. Soon people start calling up towards the stage.

'Why are you being so rude to her? She's just a little blind girl!'

'Why are some of the marbles heavier?'

'What kind of game do you think you're playing here?'

'Where's the government official?'

Gordon Spoon smiles and says something with his palms open facing the crowd, but no one can hear him. People in the audience rise from their seats and move towards the stage. Spoon turns to me and Alice and clips each of us behind the ear, swearing at the top of his voice. Alice finally pulls her hand out of the barrel with number twelve and tosses hard, hitting him right above the eyebrow. He stumbles backwards, arms flailing. There's a bit of laughter at that. She might not see anything, but Alice sure is a good shot. Just ask Laurie.

I take Alice's hand and we make a dash for it against the flow of adults now storming the stage. Gordon Spoon lunges in our direction, but we're too quick for him. We weave through the sea of bodies towards the exit, almost making it out before we get collared.

'Mum and Dad are gonna hit the bloody roof when they find out about this!'

'Georgie?'

'Can't we take you anywhere without you startin' a riot?'

Alice is behind me, still holding my hand. As soon as she realises our big brother is around she starts talking and doesn't stop to breathe. 'That Spoon bloke's a creep, he wouldn't get off my back! What they was doin' was wrong! I had to stick up for everyone! Georgie? Georgie!'

He drags us outside. Somewhere on the way out we pick up Francis and Laurie who don't say anything. Rose is waiting for us by the doors. She looks tired. 'Oh, Bats! Why couldn't you just choose a number?'

'I didn't do anythin'!'

'You both did plenty!' shouts Georgie. 'And now listen to what's goin' on in there!'

Men and women shouting, a few kids screaming over the top of everything else, probably a fistfight or two. The people now streaming out point at me and Alice. Some of them laugh at us. That's when I start crying.

'Hey, Boo, what's the matter?' says Rose.

'Are they gonna put her away?' I bawl.

'Who?'

'Alice! They want to send her away or something and now they can b'cause of this!'

'What the hell are you talking about?' says Alice.

'Bats! You've done enough swearing for one day!' says Rose. 'Boo, no one's trying to send her away.'

'Yes they are! I heard Mum and Mrs Langtry talkin' about it! Something about locking her up!'

'Aw, Boo. I'm sure you just thought that's what they were sayin'.'

'No I heard 'em!'

Now everyone except Alice is laughing at me and that only makes me cry harder.

◆

We can hear everything from the sleep-out so we all stay still, trying not to make the beds creak. Me and Alice share the little bed. Francis and Laurie get the bigger one. Georgie has his own bed at the end of ours and Rose sleeps in her own room at the back of the house. I can just make out what's happening on the other side of the door through fresh tears and a crack in the curtain. I'm sure this time that they're going to send Alice away forever.

In the living room, Mum pours tea from the china pot (not even Mrs Langtry got the china). Dad lights a pipe in his armchair. Both watch the policeman as he balances a cup and saucer on the hat in his lap.

'So what happens now?' says Dad.

'Well, nothing, Jack. They've really done nothing wrong, but I...we felt duty-bound to let you know what happened.'

'We've already heard,' Dad looks towards our room and I pull back, scared. Georgie hasn't been able to sit since he told Dad, his bum is so red and sore. We've told him we're sorry and he says it's alright, but I'm not sure I believe him.

'The people at the Golden Casket have put it down to youthful imagination,' says the policeman. 'They won't take any action, although I doubt they'll get kids up on stage again. Your Alice made a fair fool of that bloke.'

The policeman laughs. And Dad joins in! Why are they laughing? I don't understand and when I tell Alice what they're doing all she does is smile too without explaining anything.

'Where on earth did that Alice get such a suspicious mind? Has she been listening to the preachers a bit too closely?'

'Hardly! She's blind, Jim. She doesn't take anythin' at face value.'

'Well if they ever find a cure for blindness we might have a place for her on the force.'

They both laugh again.

'And, Jack? I wouldn't pay any attention to that talk around town. Don't...don't let anyone tell you what to do. Just let them be kids. Do you know what I mean?'

'Jim, I make a point of ignoring sanctimonious bastards!'

I cover my mouth in shock. Georgie is wide eyed too. Dad swore!

As the policeman prepares to leave we all close our eyes and pretend to sleep. Alice pulls the covers over our heads.

'Hey,' I say.

'Yeah?'

'Remember that bloke at the pub who gave you the ribbon?'

'Yeah.'

'Why do you reckon he did that?'

'I dunno. Maybe he just liked us.'

'He was real strange.'

'I know, he smelled bad. But if he hadn't given me the ribbon, maybe I wouldn't have got picked.'

'Maybe he was looking out for us. Like a guardian angel or something?'

'Some guardian angel! We never even got our sixpence!'

Heavens

No one came for me, to arrest me or take me away. I followed the same path as always, only this time I didn't run. My heart pounded, but I held my nerve and slowly, deliberately strolled the streets. When I reached the grounds of the Cathedral of St Nicholas, I stopped behind the church and laughed up into the sky. Already Mama's warnings were fading as though they belonged to another place now, another time.

It started with the newspaper, one of our daily rituals. Mama did try to learn English once, but not very hard. She preferred Russian.

'*Ya govoryu bez obinyakov!*'

I speak my mind.

For a long time, I took her excuse for not engaging with the local language at face value. But sometimes I did wonder what exactly she meant. Could she never articulate what she wanted to say in English? Or was she afraid of what might happen if people in this country could understand her?

She would never have read the news in Russian even if it was available, so it was up to me to buy the local paper and translate for her. Translate and filter. For Mama, what I ignored was just as important as what

I read. There was a lot of bad news and Russians—or Soviets—featured a lot. Mama did not want to know of such things.

'*Ya otvernulas ot nikh, Kolya.*'

I have turned my back on them, she once told me. When I asked why, she pretended not to hear.

The sky was a clear, deep blue. It seemed to go on forever, although I now knew its limits and that there was more out past the blue. I lay flat on the ground and allowed it all to fill my senses. The stratosphere was within reach.

I used to follow Mama's example and I tried so hard to not read anything about Soviets either. It was mostly boring stuff anyway in places that sounded so far away, like Berlin and Havana. I'd heard of these places, but I wouldn't have been able to find them on the coloured map at school. I couldn't care less what the Soviets were up to on the other side of the world. It mattered far more what they were doing here to Mama and me.

But then I read about a man named Yuri Gagarin. He went past the sky and into space and back again. At first I did not believe such a thing could occur, but story after story showed me that not only was this extraordinary feat possible, it had actually happened.

For so long I avoided any mention of Gagarin or the 'space race' or Kennedy and Khrushchev, but when it finally came out, it was Mama who started it. She pointed to a diagram of the Vostok 1 in orbit on page five of the newspaper and asked me what it was. It all came out of my mouth in a flood—Yuri Gagarin was the bravest man I had ever read about. This Russian, an air force pilot no less, was a hero. More than that, he was my hero. Mama locked the doors and hid under the bed, all the time screaming at me to stop talking, stop talking!

'*Molchi! Molchi!* Get out! They are monitoring us! Get out in the open! Go to the church!'

Why did Yuri Gagarin have to be a Soviet? It was so unfair!

A cloud drifted across the sun and I drifted under it. I could fly up into space. I could climb aboard the Vostok 1. I pictured the capsule forming around me: gigantic rocket boosters behind, ground crew scurrying far below. I felt the special suit resting on my skin and the helmet tight on my head.

I am ready for anything. I wait on the launch pad at Tyuratam, seatbelt secure over my chest and lap. Straight ahead is the morning's crisp wide blue. A few light clouds dotted here and there. And beyond that the blackness of space: a million stars and planets— heavenly bodies suspended in beautiful equilibrium. The magic takes my breath for a moment. But then I remember I have a job to do. And I have something to leave behind.

I am confident in my ground crew and the scientists working to get me here. I was chosen from the best test pilots in the USSR to become the first cosmonaut and yet there is so little piloting to do in this vehicle— everything that can be is automated. I have trained many hours for the experience of weightlessness and for the possibility that problems may occur during the flight.

Everything in my life has led me to this moment, this one beautiful moment. Ahead of me is something I cannot know yet, but very soon I will meet it head on.

Seven minutes past nine. The five rockets are firing. Can you hear them?

Wish me luck.

Poyekhali!

◆

'Hey, are you alright?'

When I opened my eyes, her face was right over mine. She smoked a cigarette and smiled broadly. I guessed she was about my age. Long red hair fell in loose ringlets around her neck and shoulders. Her skin seemed smooth and creamy, but also thin, fragile. Without the cigarette she could have been one of Mama's ornaments, but the smoke rising from her mouth and the red embers in her hand gave her an exciting, dangerous edge. I forgot all about Mama and my rocket ship and Yuri Gagarin and stood entranced by the smoke that clung to her cheeks and curled through her hair.

I wondered what it would feel like to touch that skin.

She raised her eyebrows, waiting.

'Can you hear me?'

'Yes.'

'What are you doing?'

I lay flat on the path with my legs up in the air like I was in a chair. My hands were raised in front to control the steering of my craft. But now the craft had vanished, the rockets were nothing but plain, dry earth.

'I was waiting for lift-off.'

'I think you're gonna be waiting a while!'

I could say nothing. I rolled onto my side. She wore ordinary rubber thongs that showed off her delicate feet. Just her presence made me feel sweaty and disgusting in comparison.

'So were you flying into space or what?'

I stood up, my knees covered in red dust. I towered over her.

'I was waiting to make sure there were not people behind me.'

'Behind you?'

'Following me.'

'Was anyone following?'

'No.'

She screwed her face up and said nothing for a bit.

'Who would be following you?' she said at last.

I didn't know exactly why the Soviets were after us. Mama told me they would get to her through me and that I should be on my guard all the time. I was five years old when we landed in this country: Mama, me and my father. I don't have memories of anything unusual from then. Nothing to suggest we would be holding Papa's funeral two days before my seventh birthday.

I answered the girl with something I had heard Mama say many times.

'Danger is everywhere.'

'Danger? Are you kidding? What danger?'

I remembered Mama yelling at me from under the bed that if they can send a man into space they can be *everywhere*. But in that exact moment, staring into this girl's eyes, I had no answer. No one had come for me, to arrest me or take me away.

She grinned and her eyes sparkled. 'You don't know yet, do you?'

'Know what?'

'That we're all dead!' She held a hand to her mouth and giggled.

I didn't know what to say. I scratched my neck and

swallowed.

'So you went into space,' she said.

'Huh?'

'Space. What's it like?'

She asked me the question straight and sincerely and I wondered what she must have been thinking. Was she serious? Was she really asking me about space after catching me lying on the ground with my legs up in the air? Maybe she figured anyone stupid enough to pretend to be Yuri Gagarin must know a thing or two about space.

I thought of the news reports and the details on how the Russians—the people who made Mama and me—managed to send a man outside of the earth. I thought about how it felt to shoot into orbit in my daydreams. And I gave this girl as honest an answer as I could.

'Being in space is the most wondrous experience. When you are trained to be a cosmonaut, they teach you about weightlessness by diving in water, but it is nothing like that. Imagine the water not being there and you just begin to float up from where you sit or stand. You can swim or dive or float, but you are floating in nothing, you are flying.'

She closed her eyes as I spoke and swayed her head like she was listening to music. I tingled with excitement. Shadows caressed her high forehead and cheeks. She nodded as though confirming something she already knew and paused to ash her cigarette.

'Do you know,' she said, 'when something is happening that is meant to be?'

'You mean like fate?'

'Yeah, kind of. Like when you hear a song on the radio and it's so beautiful? You just know that the song was written for you and you were supposed to hear it at exactly that moment. When the radio talks directly to you.'

'I don't know. I always thought fate can bring bad things and good things, but always for a reason.'

'I've got a good feeling about this, about you and me meeting like this. It's like we were supposed to find each other.' She held out a hand in greeting. 'My name's Carol Austin, what's yours?'

The words were on my lips—*Nikolai Andropov but call me Kolya*—but something stopped me. It was the way she asked me about space, like she really believed I had been there. At least she was far less surprised than I was at my answer.

'Yuri Aleksandrovich Gagarin.'

Perhaps Carol Austin never read the papers.

In any case, with that, I was shot into orbit.

❧

The sound is incredible. I am quite used to sitting in a noisy cockpit, but it is different this time, perhaps only because of where I'm going.

The earth is reluctant to release me from its grip and I sink back into the seat. This is not new. I have been through extreme force—up to five times that of gravity—many times before in training. The sky turns, a little like dusk, only there is no sunset and no moon rising. Slowly the blue deepens, clouds left far behind and ahead the faint flicker of what might be a star. A new burst of noise as the boosters run out of fuel and flip away to burn up in the atmosphere.

'Separation from carrier rocket completed.'

Now I am there. I am in space, where no man has been before. I take a deep breath and loosen my seatbelt.

My body drifts up and around the tight cabin. I test the food and water samples the scientists have given me without incident. I had assumed the view would be not much different to the night sky, but it is more beautiful that I could ever have imagined. The stars I have seen so often from firm ground burn brighter with piercing intensity and beauty.

And below I see my home, the place I came from.

I speak again into the radio: 'The sky looks very, very dark and the earth is bluish.'

I fly over the Atlantic Ocean and I think of my beautiful wife Valentina and our daughters Elena and Gala. Gala is only one month old. And I think of Mama. Because of the secret nature of my preparation, none of them know I am here, observing them from the heavens. And I wonder how I will tell them about this.

The match glowed in her cupped hands. She watched it intently, as though seeing it for the first time. She lit the fresh cigarette dangling from her mouth. Rather than shake the match, she pursed her lips and blew it out. The intense perfume of acrid match and rich tobacco momentarily overwhelmed me.

'Want one?' She held the packet out with one sticking out from the rest, like an advertisement. I nodded, mute, and she lit it by kissing the ends together.

'Where did you get them? The cigarettes.'

She grinned. 'Pinched 'em off my brother. He's got tons, never notices 'em gone.'

We smoked for a moment—or rather she smoked and I sucked on mine and blew smoke straight back out again, trying desperately not to choke.

'Do you live with your mother?' she said.

'Um...yes.' It seemed a stupid question.

'What about your dad?'

We had just moved into a tiny flat atop a million stairs when Papa was taken. I remember boxes everywhere as tall as me, boxes we never unpacked. Papa simply disappeared in the night. I woke up in the morning and he was not there. We couldn't give him a proper Orthodox funeral because Mama feared it would draw attention to us. Not that it mattered. We buried an empty coffin.

'He's gone.'

I didn't want to say any more and Carol Austin did not ask anything else about it.

'Did you always want to go into space?'

'Always,' I smiled. This was more comfortable for Yuri Gagarin. 'When I was younger, I read stories by Jules Verne and books about airmen. I still like to lie in the grass and watch the night sky, but I have little time to do so now with my training.'

'What are you training for?'

I stopped for a moment. I had to think about my answer. I'd forgotten sure who was answering her questions. What would he say?

'I think it will not be long before we will walk on the moon and then land on Mars. One day we will travel between planets like we do between cities today.'

'That'd be amazing.'

'It won't be far.' I leaned back. A gentle breeze picked up, rustling trees. 'One day we will travel to heaven and back.'

When Carol Austin laughed, as she did now, she

threw her head back and her hair flicked across her eyes.

'What?' I said defensively.

'How can we travel to a place we're already at?'

'What do you mean?'

'How can we travel to heaven when we're already there?'

I started to laugh with her. I thought she must love living here to think of it as heaven. But there was something about her demeanour that told me this was no joke to her. Maybe it was the way she locked eyes with me, steely hard and deadly serious.

'You think this is heaven?' I said.

'I'll tell you what I know, Yuri. There are some things I found about where we are right now and it's really hard for a lot of people to accept. But I swear to god, Yuri, this is totally the truth—don't get weird on me. There is an afterlife. I know there is because I've found out that we're in it. I am dead, or at least I died on earth some time ago. When, I don't know. But I know I'm dead and everyone here is also dead, even if they don't know it yet. You're dead, Yuri.'

I squinted at her. *She thinks this is heaven*, I thought.

She is mad!

'I'm not dead, Carol. Not yet anyway.'

'Then let me ask you this. Do you remember the exact moment when your rocket changed from being in earth to being in space?'

'Umm...' sometimes I wanted to answer as Gagarin, sometimes as myself. I felt as though I had to change costume with every turn in the conversation. 'It doesn't work like that, moving between earth and space. It happens very gradually.'

'As far as you know, you went into space and came back a hero. What I'm telling you is that you've come back to a different place from the one you left. Isn't space travel dangerous?'

'Of course! There are safety precautions and many years of research and training.'

She's crazy. I am not even Yuri Gagarin!

'Don't feel bad. Not everyone notices the passing from one world to another. I reckon most people don't.'

I stood and paced between a tree and the rear fence of the churchyard.

'Hey, I want you to turn around,' she said. 'Go on. Turn. I won't do anything horrible to you, just turn.

Now see the tree there in front of you?'

'Yes.'

'That's a Moreton Bay fig. Now I want you to look at the tree, look hard at the trunk. This might help you to understand.'

The tree was as tall as the church beside it and the branches arched almost completely overhead. The roots splayed on the ground at least as far as the branches above them, weaving in and out of the ground and over each other. On Sundays, kids made a game of jumping over them (*How many can you jump?*). My eyes followed the roots, which combined to form thick strands like rope or maybe smoke from a cigarette or the back of a rocket ship rising from the dirt.

'What am I looking at?'

'Just look, you'll see.'

I frowned, frustrated with this conversation that made no sense. She may have been pretty, but she was strange. Still, I stared at the trunk and wondered how I could leave without being rude.

Then I saw it.

Knotted and gnarled, there was a face in the

trunk. She was right, it was not obvious at first, but unmistakable. There, the thin straight nose and the large full lips. And there the thick knotted eyebrows, the narrow eyes looking back at me. I could almost make out an ear on the left side and the suggestion of a chin under those fat lips. Not an old face exactly, but not young.

'Ha, you see it!' She had moved to my side, watching me intently.

'Yes, I see.'

'You know he's different for everybody. How does he look to you?'

'What do you mean?'

'Happy? Sad?'

I stared at the face for a little longer.

'It looks...annoyed.'

Her smile dropped into a quizzical frown, but only for a moment.

'Well, we'll have to do something about that, won't we?'

'What does it look like to you?'

She leaned in close to me. The smell of dry soap fresh from the box. When she whispered in my ear my heart raced so hard I wondered if it would explode.

'You know no one's ever asked me that,' she said. 'He's never been happier.'

She kissed my cheek.

And, yes, my knees buckled under me.

'Are you okay? Come and sit here.'

I felt hot with shame and perched on a tree root, resting my chin on my hands.

'A face in a tree doesn't prove anything,' I said.

'I thought so too, but I've realised it's a sign. This is not the place you think it is and there are clues all around us that say so. Have you ever noticed that bad things never happen here?'

'Bad things happen here all the time.'

'I'm not talking about little things. Think about it, Yuri. All the really bad stuff that you read in the news or whatever. It's always somewhere else.'

We might have talked about Moscow, Washington, or London, but bad things happen everywhere. My father was still gone.

'Bad things have still happened to me.'

'But I bet the worst of it is before you arrived here. Right here.'

Where was *right here?* We moved many times after Papa disappeared, between buildings, houses, and cities. It was true that Mama hadn't talked of moving again since we arrived here. No one had come for us. I heard the ring of a tram bell from the street and the soft fuzz of the sparking pole. Spots of light filtered through the tree like searchlights. Dark shadows on the ground slithered up from the road to the wall of the church. They sharpened to reveal a man—no, two men, compact and tough—approaching us from Vulture Street.

Yuri Gagarin was in orbit for one hundred and eight minutes before he fell back to earth. He wanted to stay longer, but a hundred and eight minutes was all that was necessary to cement his legacy.

Already my craft has begun its descent. It is too soon, I tell myself. Surely there is more time. I brace myself and close my eyes for one second. Like any flight, it is more difficult to land than to get off the ground. And this flight is more difficult than most.

The retro rockets fire, slowing me down. Though

I had not noticed they were tense, my shoulders relax. I understand the source of my relief. The rockets did not always fire on command during testing.

Nothing has been left to chance. Control of the Vostok is out of my hands and with the scientists at home. I trust them with my life. The craft must re-enter the atmosphere at the right angle or it will burn up like a meteor.

I remain seated, pilot as passenger at least for now. The force now is more extreme than anything from my training and pushes me so far into the seat, I feel I will almost become part of it. Everything shakes and a tremendous roar fills my head. Outside the capsule I see flames lick the edges of the heat shield as I am buffeted through layer after layer of thickening atmosphere.

I wonder if the heat shield will hold up.

Carol Austin was the first girl I kissed. Though it was a very, very short exchange, I would long cling to the thought that her lips were the softest things mine had ever touched. I felt like I could conquer the world, like

I could leap over the Story Bridge and still have the energy to run home.

'I quite like you, Yuri.'

I wished I had never told her my name was Yuri. From the corner of my eye, shadows drew closer.

'Carol!' a voice barked.

I withdrew from her and my elation dissolved, leaving cold hard anxiety. They were not much taller than me, but broad and stocky. The family resemblance was clear.

'Carol! What's going on?'

She smiled and waved at them. 'Hi!'

'Where have you been? Dad was gonna call the cops! And who is this idiot?'

'This is Yuri.'

I smiled weakly.

One muttered under his breath, 'Oh great, this one's a fucking commie!' The other took Carol's hand and led her away around the corner of the church. 'Hey, come around here for a minute. I wanna show you something.'

'Back in a sec!' she winked at me.

When they were out of sight, the boy I assumed

was Carol's brother, the one who called me a commie, stood over me and lifted me clean off the ground by the collar.

'Listen here, you fucking little Romeo. My fucking sister is not well, not right in the head. Comprenday? She's sick and the last thing she needs is for little fuckers like you playing her for all she's worth! Stick to your own kind. And if you so much as think about her again,' at this he lowered his voice to a gravelly wet whisper and raised my ear to his mouth, 'I'll fucking kill you.'

A warm flow trickled down my leg.

He released me and I fell hard across a tree root. I scrambled backwards, willing my feet to untangle and take me as far away from this hulking creature as possible. By the time he knew I was gone, I was already at the footpath.

I ran through the streets, just like old times. I wondered how Mama would react when I told her I had wet my pants because the brother of a girl I kissed wanted to kill me. Here at last was a real enemy, an obvious threat. Now I had shouts and shaking fists behind me instead of spies, shadows, and cameras.

I was scared, terrified, but there was something else. The wind against my face was cool and fresh. The cars I dodged in and out of shone with luminous intensity.

I think I was relieved.

Until now, I knew nothing but fear. I jumped at the slightest sound. Someone banging bottles against our corrugated iron fence was enough to send Mama hiding in a cupboard and me guarding our door with a slingshot. We did nothing outside school or work, and we trusted no one but each other.

We had escaped hell to arrive in heaven, but we had never allowed ourselves to see its pleasures. Maybe the Soviets got whatever they wanted out of Papa. Maybe they had forgotten about his wife and son.

Maybe a Soviet was not something to be frightened of at all.

❧

The parachutes eject. A gentle landing and I open the hatch. If everything is right, the field should be in Takhtarova. Immediately, instinctively, I look up at the sky as blue and as crisp as it was when I launched one hour and forty-eight minutes ago.

The greeting party will not be far away. There will be celebrations. Nikita Khrushchev will know by now. For me there will be innumerable tests and investigations. And beyond that?

Suddenly I am filled with a sense of the enormity of what I have just done. My heart quickens and I feel fear for the first time since embarking on this project.

I am glad that soon I will see my family.

When I circle the craft to check for damage I hear grass rustling from behind. Expecting to see someone I know, I am surprised to find an old woman, a matryoshka in her scarf and apron. Her eyes are wide and her mouth is set in stony seriousness.

She inspects first the Vostok 1, then me in my suit.

'Have you come from outer space?'

'Yes would you believe it, I certainly have!'

At this she draws her hand to her mouth, wide eyed, and takes a step backwards. I smile at her peasant naïveté.

'Do not be alarmed, I am a Soviet.'

'Mama, why did we leave Russia and come here?'

'*Zachem eti voprosy, Babochka?*'

Babochka! I hated Mama calling me little butterfly and she knew it! I squeezed my eyes shut to stop myself from entering the wrong argument.

'Why did we come here?'

Mama stiffened, 'Your Papa worked in the Embassy. There was trouble there and Australia asked Papa if he would like to stay.'

'What kind of trouble?'

'Enough!' she screamed at me and stormed into the kitchen. She filled the sink with soapy water, even though lunch dishes were already done.

I followed her.

'Was Papa a spy?'

Mama drew a wet hand to her forehead. 'Stop! Stop!' she growled. 'You will get us both killed! They have microphones and they are waiting for any chance to catch us!'

'But it's been such a long time, Mama!'

She turned, her back to the sink, and stared at

me across the kitchen table. I wondered if she would cry. I did not know what I would do if she cried. Eventually, I realised I was worried over nothing. Her eyes remained as dry as the grass on the footpaths out the front. And when she spoke, her voice was quiet and even.

'You are so innocent, Kolya. They can wait as long as we can and they never tire. It is better if you do not know what happened right now.'

I nodded, but for the first time in my life I did not believe her. She thought I would not understand. Nothing could be further from the truth. For as long as I remembered, we had been running from make believe, a fantasy, a bogeyman.

Carol Austin was as right as anyone else.

There, in our tiny kitchen, I made a decision. Even if it meant trading one fantasy for another, I would rather live in Carol's heaven, even with her brothers in it, than Mama's paranoid hell.

'One day I will tell you the whole story.'

'What do we do until then?'

'We will drink chai and you can read me stories.'

She placed a cup and saucer in my hands, like she had

been hiding them under her skirt folds all this time and led me to the living room.

We sat in our usual places and I watched steam rise from the tea for a moment. From the bookshelf I chose our old copy of *The Cossacks* with the cover that had torn away many years before. I read, speaking Tolstoy's parts in many voices, while she sipped from her cup and grew drowsy under her crocheted blanket in her favourite armchair, always smiling at her only son.

Battle

He bristled when the publican called last drinks. Bertie had been prepared, arriving early enough to stake out a stool at the end with plenty of elbow room and a place to lean his walking stick. Now, barely forty minutes into their rationed hour of service, this bastard was calling time? He ordered another two pints and stared again at the documents laid out on the bar mat.

The letter from Rosemount was neatly typed (26/11/42), detailing ongoing care instructions for his prosthesis and the medication regimen, neither of which he had any intention of following. The other was the note he'd received not long after joining up, the same now crumpled piece of paper he had carried with him ever since. He knew every stroke of the pen, every loop in her handwriting, from the opening salvo to its inevitable, brutal end.

This is not what you were promised. Where's the glory in having a heart torn out and a limb blown apart? Where's the romance? Where's your parade?

A familiar voice cut through the throng.

'Bertie?'

He cringed, stuffed the letters back into his pocket, and slowly spun around on the stool.

'Bertie? It is you! Mate, how have you been?'

'Still alive.'

'Mate, I haven't seen you since...' Murray swayed on his feet, the slur in his voice so thick the words dribbled down his chin. 'I don't know. Basic?'

'Probably.'

'That was a fucking bitch, eh? Where'd you get posted?'

Blinding sunlight filtered through palms. Ears ringing. You're on your back. There's a commotion around. Boots trampling through thick mud, splashing dirty water onto your cheeks. You've been hit, but how? Where? A distant pain somewhere out there, beyond your body, or where your body used to be. Grabbed by the collar and dragged through the filth, head lolling from side to side as the pain comes into better focus and drives itself deeper. You cannot see for the sunlight. You cannot hear for the ringing. You cannot feel. Not anymore.

'New Guinea.'

Murray paused, allowing the words to soak in. 'Jesus,' he muttered eventually. 'You on leave?'

'Leave?'

'You're not in uniform.'

Bertie sighed and lifted his trouser leg. 'Ran into some trouble.'

Murray was sympathetic. 'Fuck me,' he muttered. 'What's this war doing to us? Everything is upside down. You know what I mean?'

Bertie nodded. Even through the alcoholic fog, Murray made a valid point.

'We're all feeling it. And these fucking Yanks everywhere, they're not helping. We're all...' he struggled to get the word out, '...*strangers* in our own town. I mean, look at this bloke.'

Bertie didn't know which bloke exactly, but there were plenty of them here in the public bar. Against a backdrop of olive drab and sepia civvies, their sharp khakis popped. Their accents cut through too, voices straight from a picture show to go with that slick, sleazy demeanour the girls couldn't get enough of. He saw it all clearly enough. A city filled with people determined to pretend like nothing was happening, like they could all cheat death itself.

'Have you seen that fucking PX?' Murray pointed across to the road to the American Postal Exchange.

'They can get anything in there: top booze, chocolate, ice cream, nylons. I saw a bloke walk out of there with a whole fucking stuffed turkey. Where are they getting turkeys from? And the girls...'

'Shut your mouth, Murray. I don't want to hear about the girls.'

'Ooooh,' Murray stretched out unsteady apologetic hands. 'Mate, mate, sorry. You're right yeah, women. Fuck 'em, right?'

An American soldier pushed his way up beside Bertie and slapped a fistful of ten-pound notes onto the bar. 'A round of drinks for everyone! It's Thanksgiving and if we can't be home, we can at least get *blind*!'

'I'm leaving,' Bertie muttered darkly. He drained the last of his beer, collected his stick and hat and made his way through the crowd, Murray taking it on himself to clear the way.

Outside the hotel was no less crowded. Drunken conversations flew around him: suggestions for which pub might still be open, laments that there was no fucking cricket, the location of the nearest brothel. He had crossed the road, Murray tagging along behind him, when the trouble broke out.

'Oi! Fucken provos! Leave the cunt alone willya!'

Two American military police were laying their batons into some kid, one of their own, a corporal judging by his stripes. A circle of Australians had surrounded them, berating the police. If the US servicemen were unpopular, the provosts were loathed and the men surrounding them were relishing the opportunity to have a go.

Murray gladly joined in. 'Hey provo!' he grinned, poking one of the police in the arse, 'Your wife says hello!'

The cop turned and scowled at Murray like a wild animal, his baton raised.

As though they had been waiting for such a signal, the mob closed in and all hell broke loose.

Hundreds of blokes streamed from the closing hotel into the intersection. They descended on the ruckus, hurling abuse at anyone in earshot. Spurred by adrenaline and a skinful, they all wanted a piece of the 'provo bastards', or any American, or anybody at all. In response, a squad of provosts stormed—ridiculously armed—out of the Red Cross building to rescue their comrades.

Bertie felt himself lifted up and carried by the surging crowd.

Into the maelstrom. It's where you belong anyway.

◆

Margaret straightened her stocking seams and sat with the girls from the typing pool who had convinced her to come along. They assumed she was heartbroken, maybe even filled with guilt, but what she felt most was relief. Other girls could wait for their men to return. She sipped her shandy through a straw, holding the glass carefully in white-gloved hands. Around her: chaos.

She couldn't deny the pace of her heart when she stepped through the doors of the Trocadero to a hot and noisy palace filled with illegal alcohol and boys. It was all so exotic and dangerous. The music was a clamour of drums and horns. Sweaty bodies danced the jitterbug, all of them going at it. And when the noise ground to an abrupt halt, the dancers clapped and cheered. A few made their way off the floor to refresh their drinks, while the rest waited for the cycle to begin again.

The girls in the next alcove reapplied their makeup in an effort to look worldly. By the bar, one of her friends tipped her glass over the head of an unlucky local lad. Margaret had been determined to maintain the face and hair of someone with perfectly prim detachment. But, watching it all, soaking it in, she knew that would be impossible.

'Don't look now,' said her friend sitting opposite, 'but I think that handsome bloke is looking at you!'

Margaret flicked her head around, startling the American boy and stopping him in his tracks. His face reddened to deep beetroot as the girls around Margaret giggled hysterically. She smiled and rose from the booth to face him, pointedly arching an eyebrow.

'Would... ah... would you like to dance, ma'am?'

He was rougher than she had assumed from a distance. The lines in his face a little deeper, eyelids a little lower. Margaret smiled. Without a word, she passed her handbag to her friends and held a hand out to her suitor.

'Lieutenant Franklin J. Miles,' he said with a slight bow. She almost giggled at his pronunciation—*loo-tenant*. 'But you can call me Frank.' At this he winked.

'Margaret Schoenberg,' she replied, hopelessly and utterly charmed, despite herself. She knew from bitter experience that an Australian, if he'd thought to say anything, would mumble—

The name's Bertie. Whaddayareckon?

     —with a pause somewhere in there to finish his beer.

Frank Miles led her to the dancefloor in time for the next song to begin. A slow number, of course. Margaret touched him timidly as they stepped through a perfunctory waltz. The band were playing a four-square beat, so their already awkward steps were hampered by unexpected beats and added shuffles.

'I'm not much of a dancer, I'm afraid,' he said.

'I'll help you where I can.'

By the third number, she was comfortable enough to remove her gloves. With her first proper touch of his hand, she noticed how callused and work-weary his skin was.

'Where are you from, Frank?'

'Staunton, Virginia, ma'am.'

'Please, if I can call you Frank, you can call me Margaret. Are you a farmer back home?'

'No ma'am. I worked in my daddy's lumberyard, but I'm hoping I can go to college after the war and learn the law.'

He had an awkward, almost hesitant way with words, but at the same time he was clearly capable. If he wanted, he would learn the law. She felt sure that Frank Miles could do whatever he wished.

❧

The sharp crack of rifle fire sent a visceral thump through Bertie's chest—

ears ringing. back on your feet, son. stay afraid or die

—echoing off the walls of the buildings and the underside of their awnings.

His leg(s) gave out as men screamed and the scuffle intensified, the dull thud of colliding bodies, fists, truncheons, boots trampling. The sound of a single man screaming made Bertie's blood run cold, the sound of pure pain and terror slicing through the mayhem. Clawing at the backs of the bodies in front of him, he sank lower to the hard stone gutter.

Let your stick go, you won't need it. You're going

down onto the pavement, onto the ground where you belong with the filth. Here's your parade, Bertie, marching right over your head.

Gripped by the collar from behind, he felt several hands drag him out from the fray to relative safety on the footpath outside the Red Cross.

'Careful mate! He's a cripple.'

Was that Murray's voice? Fuck off, Murray. Bertie was no cripple. He was more than happy to drag himself up and smash the windows of the American PX. Why not destroy something, feel the rush of taking something away from someone else? It wasn't just him. Bertie saw the same rage in the eyes of everyone here, Australian and American alike: eyes wild and rattled by war, freed from polite society, freed from attachments. To hell with king and country; he was here to defend himself, just like everyone else. One less leg changed none of that. If anything, it only sharpened his anger.

'Hey!'

Another voice this time, a beat of recognition. 'Hey, buddy. Are you okay?'

Bertie blinked at the face hanging over him.

'Jimmy?'

'Bertie! Oh my god... No uniform? You got out!'

Murray emerged from the mass of bodies, his face bleeding, holding Bertie's stick. He looked Jimmy up and down, taking in the uniform and insignia of a PFC. 'You know this bloke?' he said to Bertie, incredulous.

Bertie hauled himself back up, batting away offers of assistance.

'I was there when the blast happened,' said Jimmy. He pushed his garrison cap back and shook his head slowly. 'That was some accident.'

'You were in New Guinea with him?' said Murray.

'New Guinea?' Jimmy narrowed his eyes. 'No, we were at the Deakin yards.' He pointed a thumb in the general direction of the shipyards across the river. 'Those supply admin jerks have no idea what they're doing. I told them, didn't I, Bertie? An explosion like that was going to happen sooner or later.'

'Yeah well, guess I was the dumb bastard at the end of someone else's bad decision, right?'

'Hey,' Jimmy shuffled uncomfortably, 'you survived. And now they can't send you into combat. I mean, you're out. And we're not.'

The mob surged towards the three of them, pushing

them further down the footpath.

Murray locked eyes onto Bertie. 'You said you were in New Guinea.'

He doesn't get to look at you like that.

'Clutch harder at your pearls, Murray. I fuckin' lied, okay? Why wouldn't I? It's easier being a hero. Why do you care anyway? All you fuckin' jingo-jubes. You get trussed up in your cheap kit and your tinfoil medals and you think it hides that chip on your shoulder? We're all just counting the hours. Just part of a killing machine. Look at these fucking animals around us. You think they're heroes?'

The provosts had formed a ring around the centre of the battle, closing in, squeezing the mob. Still screaming, the man who'd been shot was stretchered out—maybe dying, maybe not. Someone had tied a shirt into a tourniquet around his thigh. Fuck. What a stupid way to check out.

A distant ambulance siren bounced up the street, drawing closer. The sound seemed to drain the energy from the rioters. Or maybe it was just the booze gripping them all harder, the humidity settling over them, fuelling a growing lethargy. With a man down, the battle subsided. Here they were, two nations' finest, throwing their hands up in disgust at the thing they had created. Tomorrow they would wake up, shake off their sore heads and crook guts, ready again to pretend they could contribute to something meaningful.

Bertie would never be one of them. He slunk away from the dissipating crowd, allowing Jimmy and Murray to fade away. He took Margaret's letter, thin and crumpled, from his pocket, held it to his nose one last time, breathing in the last of her aroma. He tore it into shreds and threw the pieces into the gutter. The next rain would wash her away.

Bertie would find some way to keep going in a world permanently upended. What else could he do?

His phantom pain twinged. Bertie leaned onto his stick and stamped his prosthesis on the ground as though the jolt would knock the pins and needles out of the timber itself.

❦

Margaret never quite made it back to her shandy. She could feel herself drawn in, absorbing every sensory detail about him. Storing it for later. The accent and the uniform were superficial; there was so much more to him. Frank Miles was a kind man, a man of simple pleasures. He was never happier than to be dancing with a nice girl after a day's hard work. He seemed to find no real difference between serving his country and serving the local Staunton community with quality building lumber or honest legal advice. He was like someone from a nostalgic past, from a picture show. She danced with Frank right up to the last number.

And after closing time?

The night was a blur of adrenaline and heat. They retreated to the small space under a house where Frank was billeted. Margaret confessed that this would be her first time. He replied: 'I'll help you where I can.' She fumbled her way through what she thought she was supposed to do, deferring to Frank when she felt most uncertain. A brief but sharp pain gave way to a slow, welling elation. She held her flushed cheek to his roughly shaven face and when it was over almost wept with the intensity of her joy. They lay together, skin to skin, waiting for the sunrise. Outside, birds chirped into the coolness of the morning.

'Margaret?'

She loved the sound of her name from his lips.

'You said that was your first time? It was mine too.'

She almost laughed at his earnest confession, like an admission of defeat. 'How would I have ever known the difference?'

'I wanted to be honest with you since I guess you're my girl now.'

Margaret felt like she could float through the ceiling.

'Are you working today?'

She shuddered at the word. 'Yes.'

'Maybe you could find an excuse not to go. I... I'm shipping out tomorrow.'

'You want me to skive off?'

'What off?'

'Call in sick.'

He smiled. 'Why not show me a good time?'

Why not, indeed. Work be damned.

❧

She stood on the platform, peering through the steam and the crowd. Reunions were happening all around: a chorus of uniforms and twirling petticoats.

Margaret was to meet someone named Dan Sullivan, a man who claimed the mantle of Frank Miles's 'buddy'. As per their arrangement, she wore a rose in her lapel, Dan wore a ridiculously unnecessary blue scarf.

Their eyes met. He smiled awkwardly.

Frank had assured her the letters would reach him wherever he was stationed. She received one reply, a short message in an unsteady hand that, between declarations of love, mentioned building an airstrip. The location had been redacted.

After that, nothing.

Doubt stalked her. After weekly letters that always failed to capture how she felt, Margaret wondered if Frank had succumbed to second thoughts. Maybe he'd chosen to forget her as a night of madness—a single night in a lifetime—and move on. They barely knew each other when they had slept together and now Margaret had unburdened herself on him: the tedium of her work, her shallow friendships, her frustrations with Australia, her dream of leaving with him. Too much, too soon. And Frank no doubt harboured his own dreams. Perhaps a beautiful southern gal with whom he would have a brood of Betty-Sues and Bobby-Joes. By the time she gave up waiting for a reply, Margaret had convinced herself. She wished Frank nothing but love and happiness.

Then a letter out of the blue, postmarked US Services, but not from Frank.

'Dan?'

He nodded and approached cautiously, sweating, his grin hardened to a grimace.

'I'm Margaret.'

He offered her a deferential bow, an instant reminder of Frank's gentlemanly mannerism. Margaret ached.

'I thought this was something I should do in person. It seemed too important to just throw in the mail.'

'I understand.'

'I can't spare much time. Is there somewhere we can go?'

They strode down the hill to the Shingle Inn and settled into a corner booth. Dan ordered them tea.

'Well,' he said, reaching into his jacket, 'here it is.'

Between his fingers, Dan held out a small ribbon, yellow with stripes of red, white, and blue. It was frayed at the edges. Margaret took it in her hand and stared at it.

'It's his service ribbon.'

The drinks arrived and the dark interior of the room pressed in on her from all sides.

'I... I'm glad I found you,' Dan almost whispered. 'I'm only here for a few days before I leave for home.'

'He told you about me?'

'All the time. He drove us all nuts talking about this Australian girl he'd met and about how he was going to come back here after the war and take you back to Virginia.'

Margaret ran her fingers over the ribbon. In its textures, its fibres, she could sense his presence.

'What happened to him?'

Dan sighed.

'Please.'

'We were only a few days in, just north of Port Moresby. It was an ambush, just... chaos. Everyone was getting hit, Frank was right out the front. Tore his legs up pretty badly. He fought hard, but the stretchers didn't make it back to the medics in time.'

The first tears in a long time carved cool lines down Margaret's cheeks.

Dan reached across the table and placed a hand over hers. 'Before we shipped out, we swapped our ribbons and made a promise to each other in case one of us didn't make it back. I promised him I would find you.'

Margaret nodded.

'He was a good man, Margaret, a hero.'

She took her hand away from his and covered her face. She cried for Frank. She cried for their shared dream and the meaninglessness of it being taken from them. War and circumstance brought them together and ripped them apart. What was she to make of that? She had lost her man, the only man that ever mattered to her. She had lost a piece of herself.

Margaret allowed herself to cry for all that loss and sorrow, just that once.

◆

The tram slowed to complete stop near Edward Street, surrounded by a growing sea of joyous faces and dancing bodies.

'What a day!' cried a man, brandishing the evening paper like a barker. A single word splashed the front page:

PEACE!

It had been the word on everyone's lips since May, but months dragged on and further horrors apparently had to be unleashed before it could apply outside Europe.

Bertie carefully descended the steps of the stalled tramcar. Around him, people tore strips out of the newspaper and threw it into the air like streamers. Men had climbed on top of the building awnings, others hung from traffic lights. An impromptu march had begun down Queen Street, heading nowhere as far as Bertie could tell. The breeze lifted the paper high in the air, creating flurries of paper snow.

A group of women began to sing *Wonder When My Baby's Comin' Home.*

Even from across the street, through the swamp of bodies, she was unmistakable. Her eyes flashed as she took in the scene, her hair pinned up but with loose strands framing her perfect face, the same maroon coat she wore when he first took her to the Trocadero. That night she wore it buttoned right up to her throat, today she wore it open.

For a short, panicked moment, he lost her as she

crouched down. He began to cross towards where she had been, charting a bumbling path through vacuous, lumpen faces desperately soaking in the manic hedonism they mistook for joy.

'Margaret!'

No way she could have heard him now that an obnoxious trumpeter had begun tossing unsteady melodies down from a high window: *God Save the King*, *It's a Long Way to Tipperary*. People were now waving flags, endless recombination of the same tired reds, whites, and blues: Australia, Britain, New Zealand, America.

Through a brief opening in the crowd, he caught sight of her again, just as she lifted the child onto her hip. His eyes popped and his heart thumped harder. He stumbled after them, using the stick to steady himself as he was buffeted on all sides. Margaret's hint of a smile suggested she was quietly pleased with the events unfolding. The child clung tightly, sometimes looking up and out at the festivities, sometimes burying her face into Margaret's shoulder.

'Margaret!'

This time, he was close enough for her to hear. The

shock of recognition wasn't the response he expected. He smiled and waved. She wrapped her arms around the child and backed away from the street, away from him.

'Margaret! I just want to talk!'

He lunged towards the footpath, pushing revellers out of the way, cracking their shins with his stick. By the time he reached the spot on the corner where she had locked eyes with him, she was already gone. He paced a tight circle, sweat soaking his shirt, gasping for breath, unsure which direction to head. A flash of maroon disappearing around the corner and he took chase, hobbling after her, wading through paper snowdrifts, phantom pain searing deeper into his thigh.

He pushed against the current as more people arrived, all of them chanting:

'VICTORY! VICTORY! VICTORY!'

The music had now moved onto *The Star-Spangled Banner*.

Exhausted and doused in sweat, Bertie staggered into the crowd, slashing his stick at anyone who dared get in his way. He found a short bench and threw himself down. Tears of frustration and disgust ran down his face.

She was gone. Why did he want to talk to her anyway? What would he have even said? Her coat fluttered away on the breeze like so much of yesterday's news. Who was she anyway? Who was that child? Who was he? They were all just bodies among the thousands filling out an increasingly unfamiliar place, an artifice that served no better purpose than chasing ghosts.

'VICTORY! VICTORY! VICTORY!'

He glared at the ecstatic faces surrounding him, all of them trapped in an eternal present. Not one of them had given a thought to what would happen tomorrow because they were out of the habit. Maybe that would change. Maybe not.

Some historic moment.

It's just one damn thing after another.

Gifted

The phone alerted him again. Marcus sat back on the stairs and unlocked his screen as the children played around him. A couple of kids had climbed up behind him where a window looked out to the library's forecourt. He heard them laughing and doing blowfishes on the glass. To his left, a row of more studious-looking kids sat at computers with oversized coloured keyboards and track balls. They attempted a literary variation of Tetris—stacking letters to form words which pop into nothingness as soon as they form—except most of the kids here were preliterate so they just raced each other to stack random letters to see who could lose first (and therefore win, presumably).

He opened the message. It was Eleanor, again.

—Are they there yet?

He replied:

—Nope.

At the other end of the room, a slide show ran through a long loop of children's artwork: some scribbles, some representative, a few genuinely beautiful. In the corner, a group of boys constructed increasingly elaborate forts from foam blocks, admired their handiwork for a moment, then suddenly (maybe at some undetectable signal) charged into it headfirst, pro-wrestling style.

Charlie was oblivious to it all. She kneeled at the small solitary bookshelf and stared at it, that unsettling stare when she lapsed into one of her reveries. She waved one hand across the spines of the books and held the other below as though catching the dust that fell. She lifted her hand and inspected it for a moment, before stuffing it into her pocket. Marcus smiled. She insisted any new clothing have plenty of pocket space. This presented a challenge for a girl her age—Eleanor had sewn big patch pockets onto today's yellow summer dress—but Charlie insisted it was necessary, even though she rarely carried any actual things (other than dust bunnies) in them. Marcus thought of the behaviour as endearing, though not everyone agreed.

'Where is she? Where is that little special girl of mine?'

Charlie snapped out of her daydream and leapt up, scanning the room. 'Mum?'

'Chaaaarrrrlaaaaaaheeeee!'

Marcus had never known Tanya to be quiet, but something about this new boyfriend of hers had amped her voice to a shrill wail, even in regular conversation. He suspected, from her tone alone, that Whippo would not be far behind.

He observed their arrival from the other side of the room.

'I don't know why we had to meet here,' she said. 'Lie-baries give me the creeps.'

'Is this even a library? There's, like, kids and screaming and noise and shit. Where are all the books?'

'It's the kids section. This is what they do now because kids don't read books anymore.'

Whippo contemplated this as Charlie rushed to them, wrapping her arms around her mother's legs.

Tanya lifted the child into her arms and the pair shared a chest-crushing hug with claims and counter claims of who has missed the other more.

'Hey Dorkus,' said Whippo, looking to where Marcus stood.

Marcus responded with a curt nod. 'Where have you been?' he said to Tanya.

'We had to park at the arse end of nowhere. Why

did you want to meet here anyway? It's chaos with all this bloody rain.'

'I wanted to bring Charlie somewhere she would like.'

'Somewhere we can't afford to park.'

'You could have taken public transport.'

'Whippo doesn't like public transport,' she said. Whippo nodded in confirmation. 'He doesn't like putting his arse where someone else's has been.'

'That must get exhausting.'

'It was stupid coming here. Haven't you been watching the news?'

There had been talk of flooding if the rain didn't ease up, but Marcus hadn't thought much about what that might mean for today's handover. He had been thinking more about the conversation and how he could broach the topic. He needed somewhere like this to keep Charlie distracted and noisy enough to allow the adults to thrash it out. There was no room to account for breaking riverbanks. They would just have to deal with that if it became a problem.

Tanya lowered Charlie back to the floor. 'Okay my darling girl, go and play with the other kiddies for a second, then we'll go.'

Charlie turned her nose up and squinted at her mother. Marcus decided this was either in response to the babyish tone of Tanya's voice or the assumption that Charlie would deign to play with other children. She returned the to the bookshelf and removed a picture book. She brushed at the pages, as though clearing something away from them.

'Did you get my message?' Marcus said to Tanya.

'What message?'

'About Charlie.'

'What about her?'

'I wanted to pick her up early next week.'

Tanya stiffened. 'We agreed. One week each. Last time I checked that was seven full days. When you want more time with her, you tell me three weeks in advance.'

'I sent you an email four weeks ago about this.'

'Didn't get it.'

'I put a read receipt on it.'

'Must have been someone else. I've changed my email address. The old one got hacked.' She emphasised the last word, as though showing off something new she had learned.

'Hacked? Don't bullshit me, Tanya. It's just a day early. It was the only time I could get in to see the psychologist.'

'She doesn't need a psychologist. She's not crazy!'

'She's a bit weird,' murmured Whippo.

'Whose side are you on?' cried Tanya.

'Mine.'

She rolled her eyes. 'Go and get us a coffee or something. I'll come out with Charlie in a second.'

Whippo shuffled out of the room.

'We need to help her, Tanya. Charlie is gifted.'

Tanya scoffed. 'Gifted.'

'I'm serious.' Marcus said. 'She's on level thirty readers and she's still in prep for shit's sake. The teachers are saying they've never seen anything like it.'

'So she's smart. What's wrong with that?'

'Nothing. But she needs to be assessed.'

'For what?'

'So she can be challenged. They think she plays with imaginary things because she's bored.'

They were arguing again. They were such nice people, all of them. Even Whippo was great sometimes, eating cereal in front of the TV with her or letting her wander through the neighbourhood looking for interesting words. Nice people, as long as they weren't together.

The argument was over her. It was always over her. They said something about her being 'gifted'. Charlie wasn't sure if that was a good thing or a bad thing. She turned the word over in her mind. Gifted. She shrugged to herself. It was just a thing.

She checked her pockets again. A few names, some 'doing words' as her teacher calls them, little words like 'if' and 'it'. Charlie collected as many as she could from the bookshelf, but places like this were not great. Inside a library and especially in a children's section there wasn't much to find. Other kids held their words, they were careful with them, kept them close to their chests. Most of them didn't have all that many words so every new one was something rare and precious. They weren't always sure what to do with them, but jealously guarded them anyway.

Adults, they were the complete opposite. They threw words around, wasted them, stepped on them, treated them like toys, and discarded them without a second thought. They would shoehorn words into each other whether they belonged together or not. They smeared words over whatever surfaces were available. They would slice them, smash them. Adults didn't seem to like words at all.

Charlie used to get upset at this, until she realised something very important. Neither the adults nor the children could see what they were doing. Only she could actually see the words.

Her parents resumed their usual activity, sharpening their phrases and throwing them at each other. They raised their voices and spent words fell around them. Charlie was reminded of a war movie Whippo once let her watch. A man fired a machine gun and the empty shells bounced off the ground to form piles at his feet.

The words at her parents' feet didn't last long. Some of the younger kids circled around, absently gathering every word as fast as they were made. They knew the value and picked up everything. Even the words they were not supposed to know. Especially the words they were not supposed to know.

Charlie decided to see what else she might find. Outside the kids section, lounge chairs and tables were crammed with people at laptops. Almost all of them wearing headphones. She wandered through the space, taking in the scene. It was busy, people moving between the ground floor rooms and the open atrium that led to the upper levels. Lots of activity but not many words. She checked under desks, in the back of armchairs. These were usually great places to find loose phrases. Nothing. Frustrated, she sighed and ran a hand idly along a rack of hanging newspapers. It seemed to her that people who worked in libraries were as good as kids at tidying up strays.

)

'This is not about you,' Marcus hissed.

His face was bright red, though more from embarrassment than anger. It seemed his plan to have this discussion in a noisy place wasn't as well thought out as he'd hoped. The room was noisy, but not even a couple of dozen playing children could match Tanya's screeching.

'It's not about you either! This is about Charlie getting a normal life.'

Around them, the other parents were herding their own youngsters away. One mother drew her nappy bag closer, as though shielding herself. Other parents bent down and ushered their charges, preparing to leave. Marcus could see they were causing a scene and everyone around them was too embarrassed to intervene.

'A normal life? What's so normal about what you're offering her, Tanya? That douchebag boyfriend of yours is not exactly a model for parenting. You let her stay up all night, eat shitty food, watch inappropriate movies. If she wasn't so mature, you'd have broken her already. As it is she comes back to me addled.'

The mutters around them grew louder and the room began to thin out. *Come on, we're going.* Bags and protesting children were dragged towards the exit.

'What about that little piece you've shacked up with then? What kind of model is she? All those precious books and vases and trinkets she keeps on the shelf. How is Charlie supposed to be a kid when she can't touch anything in your house?'

This was their regular dance, back and forth, raking over the coals of a brief but productive relationship. Every slight, every nasty aside, every cold response was catalogued and reviewed. By now it had become a recitation.

It wasn't until the last of the others had left the children's corner that they noticed the thump at the window. Whippo curled his fist and beat desperately at the glass from outside, his voice raised, but muffled.

Tanya and Marcus broke their dance to stare at him.

'What's he saying?' said Marcus.

'Something about a radio,' said Tanya. 'What about it?' she yelled through the glass.

'Wfffr fucking rrrruuh! Now! Waaagaah ohhhna fucking air! Woo!'

'Did he say he was just on the air?'

Tanya nodded.

'What for?'

'I don't know.' She raised her voice to cut through the glass. 'What for?'

'Fucking flood, baby! They wanted someone to sound panicky! Yeah man!'

Marcus looked around. The commotion wasn't

confined to their corner of the library. People everywhere were streaming out of the place. Those who weren't had gathered at the windows overlooking the river. Even the headphone-and-laptop types had unplugged and were taking photos.

'Nice work, Marcus. Bringing your daughter into the most dangerous place in the city. Real smart.'

'Oh shut up, Tanya. Charlie! Let's get going!'

They looked down to the bookshelf where Charlie had been.

'Charlie?'

Tanya spun around. Marcus squinted at the crowd by the window.

'She can't have gone far. She was just here.'

'CHARLIE!'

Marcus ran from the children's corner, happy to leave Tanya to rely on the potency of her voice. Likely, Charlie had been drawn to the crowd and was somewhere in that sea of legs. No big deal.

♦

The librarians looked worried. Nothing especially

surprising about that. Charlie hadn't seen library people that much, but whenever she did, they had sad eyes and wrinkles on their foreheads. It seemed a shame to Charlie that they would feel like that all the time. Today was different though. The sky was dark and everyone here wore a librarian frown as they bustled through the forecourt,

out to look at the river

'It's broken the bank.'

in to escape bursts of rainfall

'Traffic is jammed over the bridges.'

around in circles, holding phones aloft.

'Network's down.'

The crowded space and tense energy reminded Charlie of when she went to sideshow alley and her Dad wrote his phone number on her arm in black texta in case she 'got away'. Numbers were really important to him. Sometimes she wished she could see numbers the way she saw words.

Charlie sidled up to a pair of adults—a short, stocky man and a taller, flustered-looking woman—staring out at the rain, debating whether to make a run for the bus station. A string of words, tangled into a messy half-sentence, dangled from the man's phone. Charlie couldn't make out any of the individual words, but a clump like that usually contained interesting or hard-to-find words. The phone was in a case attached to his belt: very practical and tantalisingly close. In straining to look over the shoulders of the people standing in front of him, the man danced back and forth. The words swayed along with him. Charlie stood still by his side, watching from the corner of her eye. With one quick move, she snatched the clump and stuffed it into her pocket. The man stopped jiggling and looked down at her.

'You right, kid?'

She smiled. They always liked it when she smiled. 'Yes, thank you,' she said.

The man turned his attention back to peering over the shoulders of the people in front of him and said to the woman, 'Fuck it, I reckon we should make a break for it now.'

'It's only going to get worse from here,' she replied.

Charlie waited to see what they might do, but they remained standing there, in silence, staring.

Something very important was happening, but Charlie could not understand what it was. She turned away from the crowd and looked up. Not many people look up, but sometimes it's worth looking for the lovely things above. It was a nice space, a high atrium stacked with open balconies and floors. Her Dad once showed her where she could find the lifts. Maybe if she got up high, she could see what everyone was looking at. If she was really lucky, she might find a few words for her collection along the way.

❦

Searching? Searching? Are they serious? Bloody technology. The one time you need—absolutely need—a phone to work, the bars conveniently vanish and in their place one word and a string of dots to suggest that civilisation is just out of reach. Just wait a little longer...

Marcus dashed through the crowded forecourt, avoiding Whippo coming the other way, triumphantly holding two lattes over his head. No sign of her. He sprinted to the information desk by the lifts. No one there.

No, of course not.

His heart raced and his hands shook. He took a deep breath and attempted to scan the area systematically. Unsuccessful. His eyes darted left and right; every reflection, every flash of yellow was her, almost her, surely her.

'Sir, are you alright?'

In the blur of bodies, Marcus didn't even register the uniform. Any offer of help was welcome as far as he was concerned. 'My daughter. She was just here. I thought she was here.'

'Sir, calm down. What's her name?'

'Charlotte. Charlie. She's Charlie.'

'And when did you last see her?'

Marcus stopped and thought for a second. When had he last seen her? How long had he been arguing with Tanya before they realised the only thing they had worth arguing over was gone?

'Um, I don't know. Not long. Not long at all.'

'Can you give me an estimate? It makes all the difference.'

'Ten minutes? Tops. Her mother is here too. She'll be looking. And screaming. Screaming and looking.'

In his mind he ran through everything he should have been doing: stay still, stay calm. A nauseous lurch flowed through him as he realised what he was responsible for: his daughter, barely past five years of age, wandering unsupervised in a tremendously crowded public space in the middle of some mad tumult. He gave the security guard Charlie's basic details and appearance.

'She's smart! She's really, really smart.'

He wasn't quite sure why he'd said that. Why that was important. Maybe he was saying it to himself. He dashed through the throng of bodies, an endless parade of random people chattering, bustling, and dawdling. The rain eased and the crowds were dispersing: some getting as far away from the river as possible, others moving closer to gawp. A clawing, gasping panic began to overtake him. The seconds passed, each one taking her further from him.

❧

On the ceiling, someone had placed giant bugs. Christmas beetles. Not real ones, they were big brown metal things. They didn't move, only watched what was happening below.

Finding the lifts wasn't too difficult, but Charlie was concerned she might be too short to reach the buttons. Sometimes to get high up, you had to be tall first. But this elevator was fine. She couldn't reach the top button, but the one below was okay. Not much in the way of words in here either. Yes, she decided these librarians must be *diligent*. That was a nice word she picked up outside the teachers' room at school. She looked at the label next to the button she'd pressed.

Special collections.

Okay. She would go to special collections and see what she could find. After a satisfying ping, the doors slid shut in front of her and carried her as high as she could go.

Helicopters buzzed close overhead, rattling windows. A few rays of sunlight cut through a break between heavy, brooding clouds.

'Spooky,' said Whippo, taking a sip of coffee. 'We gotta get the fuck outta here.'

'We haven't found Charlie.'

'Dorkus is looking for her. He'll text you when he finds her.'

'Nigel, do you seriously think I'm going to leave without finding my daughter?'

'Don't call me Nigel.'

Tanya had never really paid attention to the river until now. She knew it was there, of course, but how often do you stop and stare at the millions of litres flowing past? Now she stopped. And stared.

The water had a hypnotic swirl. It eddied and sloshed and plumed and wrestled with itself. Wells would rise up, propelled by some unseen force below, disgorge their watery content, attempting to reach skyward, before running out of steam and settling back into the opaque brown maelstrom only for another plume to rise somewhere else. It never settled. It never stopped. And it was loud.

'Fuck me!' said Whippo. 'Look at that.'

A long sexy speedboat, a millionaire's toy, had wedged itself into one of the bridge's pylons.

◆

A few people were around on this floor, but for the moment no one paid Charlie much attention. She wondered where she could find the windows overlooking the river.

This level was nothing like the others she had seen. The others had rows and rows and rows of books, more than the school library could ever hold. Charlie spent a lot of time with books. Books helped her make sense of the words she saw everywhere. They helped her understand how words go together and what they look like when people order them. Books were okay. But the way others talked about them, Charlie wondered if she was missing something.

'I love books,' said her teacher in the first week of prep.

'Why?' said Charlie.

'Because books open up a whole world of possibility. Books are a window into...'

Charlie lost track somewhere around there. It wasn't the only time she'd heard stuff like that. A window? What did that even mean? For her, books were useful, but the words in them were dead. Out here, words did all sorts of things. They combined and split apart, moved around and re-formed. They turned up in strange and wonderful places. They were never still.

But this floor was not filled with rows and rows of dead words. This floor looked more like a shop for antiques. And one antique caught her eye.

It was a large white vase with a picture on it painted blue: birds facing each other, dancing together in silence, surrounded by strange looking trees and buildings. It was pretty.

And inside it was stuffed full of words. Real ones, not the dead kind from books.

Charlie stared at it. All the words she had ever found were on the ground, left behind on tables, hanging sadly from someone's belongings. Everything from her collection was someone else's junk. She'd never thought to look somewhere special.

Special collections.

An amazing thought occurred to Charlie. She took a deep, measured breath in. Her fingers and toes tingled with pins and needles.

Someone had put those words in there.

There are other people like me.

Someone like her had kept their own collection and

stored it in a white vase with blue dancing birds painted on it. What kind of words deserved such gentle and careful treatment? They must be words she had never encountered before. What's more, someone—the same someone who collected them?—had placed the vase out there in the open, just out of reach. Charlie inched her way closer, reaching, desperate to know what such precious words must feel like.

'Hey there!'

Charlie jumped in fright and whirled around to find herself face to face with someone official. She wanted to run away, but she didn't want to leave the words in the vase without touching them.

'Hey, it's okay! You look very lost there, sweetheart!'

She wasn't old like a lot of the librarians Charlie had seen. She was probably younger than Charlie's mum.

'What's your name?' she asked.

'Charlie.'

'Charlie, I'm Sam. Are you missing your mum or dad?'

Charlie blinked at her. Mum and Dad would still be talking, still surely flinging their arguments at each other's faces. They always took a long time doing that.

Charlie wasn't worried.

'Neither. They're downstairs.'

Sam frowned for a moment and smiled again. 'I think they'll be looking for you, Charlie. Everyone is going home now. Let's go down there and see if we can find them.'

She held a hand out. Charlie crossed her arms.

'Sweetheart, we have to go. You can't stay here.'

'No!' Charlie was happy to go once she'd had a closer look at the words in the vase. She wasn't sure how to say that. She backed away instead, turned, and lunged at the table, desperate to be closer to the vase, to see what was inside. She knocked it with the back of her hand and watched wide eyed as it rocked back and forth—once, twice—before falling on its side and rolling towards the edge. A few words tumbled out, but Charlie couldn't make out what they were.

Sam cried out and pushed past, clawing at the vase with her fingertips. Charlie fell backwards onto her bottom. As the vase fell through the air, a few of the lighter, more airy words fluttered out like ash fragments from a fire. And when it finally hit the ground— *SMASH!*—its contents shattered, sending particles scattering across the polished concrete.

Sam dropped to her knees, her face white, her mouth open, staring at the dust and fragments of something that had once formed part of a special collection.

Charlie squinted at the words that mingled in the wreckage, but her excitement was short lived. Why was this thing deserving of the name 'special'? Charlie wouldn't have considered anything in the vase special. It had contained no treasures, nothing puzzling, none of the kind of words she liked to turn over in her hands and investigate further. These were words that could have come from anywhere: doing words, naming words, even little words like 'if' and 'it'. Who would have collected something like this? For what purpose? None of them even went together particularly well. They couldn't form sentences or even phrases.

Sam sighed and pushed a few shards around with the toe of her shoe before turning back to Charlie.

'Why did you do that?'

Charlie didn't wait to answer. A question like that was a precursor to trouble. She jumped to her feet and ran, found the stairs, and dashed down them as fast as she could. Maybe she had missed something. Maybe the words were more valuable than they appeared to be.

This was the kind of thing her parents would find out about. Everyone was going to be angry with her. And they would use this as an excuse to get even angrier at each other. From somewhere below, her mother's voice rang up from the atrium.

'Where's my daaaawwwwtaaaaaaah?'

Charlie couldn't stand the thought that her parents might turn their angry words on her. At least with each other they couldn't see what was coming at them.

❧

She stopped at the bridge railing, unnoticed by the people around her. They had their own problems. They were all trying to leave, marching quick step. Those who could shouted into their phones about transport and helicopters. It wasn't doing them any good. The wind lifted their words up over the bridge and they slowly tumbled down to the water.

Debris from upriver was being carried out to the bay: mostly unidentifiable plastics, kids' play equipment, camping gear, eskies.

She watched a couch drift by.

She had been thinking about the words in the vase and about her own collection at home. Unlike the books in the library, Charlie didn't keep anything ordered. She just liked to have them around her. She liked to think she looked after them too. Maybe the vase in special collections was filled by someone who thought the same way. And now it was ruined. One small stupid act from Charlie and it was gone.

But the words that it contained still troubled her. She could see the sense in collecting rare words, but why keep ordinary words like that?

A new thought occurred to her. Maybe keeping them wasn't the right thing to do.

Charlie reached into her pockets and removed the few words she had collected in the library. She turned them over in her hands, watching the sunlight strike them. During their time in her pocket, they had rubbed up against each other. A couple had clung together in awkward compound words. One of them had even attracted un ugly 'LY' at the end. They were always doing that.

'Charlie!'

Her Dad's voice drew closer, carried on the breeze from somewhere behind. Charlie would have to brace herself for trouble.

No, adults didn't seem to like words at all. They abused them, threw them around, left them wherever they pleased. But maybe that was what you're supposed to do with them.

Best to get this done now.

Charlie stood on tiptoes, reached over the handrail, and let the words fall. The flood claimed them. They spun and twisted on currents, crashed into each other and broke into pieces before they were finally taken under. Maybe they would settle to the bottom of the river, maybe they would drift out to sea.

Maybe one day she might see them again.

Rosaries

It didn't rain when I watched you go into the ground today. The sun cut through the crisp spring air, the sky clear and wide. Stiff grass coiled under my feet. Down the short road from the ceremony, a row of jacarandas formed perfectly round purple ponds between headstones and obelisks.

I don't know what I expected. That in itself is strange. This was a scene I'm sure I had replayed over and over in my dreams. Was the earth supposed to work itself into a tempest, tectonic shifts and lightning strikes? How did my imagined self behave? How did she feel? Wasn't she supposed to be happy? My fantasies of this moment had disappeared like so much smoke.

Here it was. Happening right before me.

And I felt nothing at all.

Except that's not exactly right. What I felt was an acute absence of anything. My husband of twenty-seven years was being laid to rest and not a single emotion seemed appropriate.

Maybe I had exhausted my allocation of emotions when you were alive.

❧

You probably don't remember the morning that set all this in motion.

I had a routine worked out, step after step neatly compartmentalised and hard won. I was never naturally methodical, I learned to make myself that way. I woke before dawn in complete silence. No alarm so as not to disturb you. I wrapped my dressing gown around me and scurried past the bedroom mirror, avoiding my reflection. I had no desire to see what had happened to that woman, the deterioration in her skin, her eyes, what new scars she had acquired.

At some point in a long distant past, the absolute silence of the morning was a sounding board for planning my escape. Remember the time I left for a week and a half? Of course you do. Night after night you stood outside my parents' house, drunk as a lord, screaming my name into the dark, at first throwing bricks into the windows until the aggression and threats gave way to tears and elaborate declarations of love. I never gave you enough credit for knowing exactly what buttons to push. I only returned home because of what you and your mates did to my father. We all saw the bruises and the cuts, that was no secret, but there was something else, something awful. Dad never spoke about it, not even to Mum.

I never completely abandoned the habit of fantasising escape, you know. A woman can dream, can't she? I could change my name, go into hiding. I could hide my whole family: parents, sister, nephews. I knew if I tried to leave again, none of them would be safe. In my mind though, we could all vanish in a puff of smoke and you'd be left with nothing. How could I convince them to do that for me? My sister always said you were my problem; washed her hands of it all years ago. I guess she never wanted to get that knock on the door to face a group of your disgusting cronies from Licensing Branch. I don't blame her.

Still, it was a lovely dream.

I prepared your breakfast, exactly the way you liked, ready at ten minutes past six when you threw yourself down at the kitchen table, spread the paper across the fake wood laminate, lit your second cigarette for the day, turned the radio on as loud as it would go and began shovelling oily bacon and eggs into your tiny mouth.

I stood back beside the kitchen door and waited, only the most furtive glances in your direction.

You had your brown suit on that day, the expensive one from George Symons, for a court appearance probably. The bulge under your left arm was noticeable only if you were staring, only if you knew. From your bedside table at night to the vanity while you showered, you never parted with it. Keep it loaded and leave the safety off. That was your motto, wasn't it? I picked it up once, you know, while you were sleeping, felt the dull grey metal, ran my fingers over the barrel, the handle, the trigger. I pointed it at you in bed, lined the sights up between your eyes. Heart hammering in my ears, limbs tingling.

I shook off the memory.

Though you ate and smoked and read and listened as usual, I noticed an anxious energy about you on this day. You hunched and shrugged your shoulders, shifted in your chair, cracked your knuckles and rubbed your fists in your lap. Your face reddened. These were the kind of signs I usually saw late at night, when you arrived home full of American bourbon.

'Fuck it,' you muttered.

'Sorry?'

'You deaf? I said, fuck it. FUCK. IT.'

I blinked. 'What's wrong, Johnno?'

'You don't know what's wrong? Are you stupid or lying?'

The hairs on the back of my neck stood to attention and I barely held down the rising panic clawing its way up my throat. 'I don't know what you're talking about.' I tried not to let my voice quiver. I took a step back into the screen door. 'I really don't.' The thought turned over and over in my head: how is this possible? I had followed the rules. I had done everything right.

You slammed your fist down, lifted the plate from the table and flung it at the floor. It smashed into shards of glazed ceramic, greasy streaks across the linoleum. You pushed your chair back and waved a dismissive hand in the direction of the food.

'Eat it.'

'Eat it?'

That smirk. That hateful, nauseating smirk followed me as I crouched to the floor and with shaking fingers picked up a small piece of bacon and put it in my mouth.

'Keep going.'

I attempted to eat a glob of egg white that ran through my fingers and dribbled down my chin. I tasted nothing but bitter dust.

'Well?'

'I don't know what's wrong.'

'I provide for you, I put up with your bullshit, and the only thing I ask is that you listen to me. When I say eggs over easy, I mean over easy. Last time I checked that didn't mean so dry its sticks in the back of my throat. Now eat the rest of that shit and cook my breakfast again. Properly this time.'

'*What?*'

I know. It wasn't what I said, of course, but how I said it. The word escaped more through a single moment's exasperation than anything. It was a small slippage in the armour I had built around myself.

I'm sure you remember what happened next. Or maybe you don't. That split second of recognition shared between us: you glimpsed a part of me you hadn't reached. And your eyes crystallised into white rage. You grabbed me by the throat and pinned me high against the wall. You pressed the gun to my temple so hard it was bruised for weeks.

Weeks? Maybe it was months.

'Sometimes you women need to be taught a few lessons to keep you in line.' You shook your head like you were disappointed in me, but the smirk had returned and it would harden with each pull of the trigger, each click.

One. *Hail Mary.*

Two. *Full of grace.*

Three. *The Lord is with thee.*

Four. *Blessed art thou amongst women.*

Five. *And blessed is the fruit of thy womb, Jesus.*

'There's one bullet in here, bitch. Looks like it's your lucky day.'

Lucky day or not, it didn't stop you from using your fists.

Even through swimming consciousness I knew you were sorry. You told me constantly. You lay next to me, one arm and one leg over me inadvertently sending rips of pain through my entire body. You sobbed. It wasn't you; it was the drink, it was work. There was an internal inquiry. Maybe a Royal Commission. You were in trouble and you took it out on me. You knew it was wrong, but I talked back to you. I knew how you hated that. It was no excuse, but I should've known better. You loved me. You hoped I could find it in my heart to forgive you.

This was your pattern. Beat me within an inch of my life so I want nothing more than for you to finish the job, then stop. Leave me on the floor for a while. Come back and feel awash with remorse at the pathetic, barely human thing crawling to the bathroom on her belly.

We had an arrangement. Unspoken, but you knew the rules as well as I did. My safety had been built on a foundation of routine. For years I had refined every interaction with you to the smallest detail. Eggs? I made *everything* to your precise demands.

And then you thought you could change it all on a whim?

I was foolish to think that some magic formula could placate you. You would always find a way to take your frustrations out on me, even if you had to invent a reason.

Your instincts, though, they were right. You suspected something had changed. You begged my forgiveness, placed yourself at my mercy, even appealed to what was left of my faith. But I had already detached. I had to find a new way to survive. And if there is any advantage to being bedridden for weeks, it's that it gives you time to think.

You were nothing if not regular. Sunday mornings I watched your pious face sing hymns to a god you didn't believe in. Sunday nights were a long attempt at arousal before slapping me around. Weekdays began with a strenuous climb to work at the Spring Hill station; lunchtime a few beers; and later a drunken stumble back to catch a train home, alone, sometimes muttering. Maybe you thought you could sober up a little by walking back.

I took the time to observe you and I had the routine down. That shortcut through the park down Jacob's Ladder: eighty-four stairs, broken by the nine landings, in the shadow of the old convict-built mill. I once heard about this fellow, three sheets to the wind, who fell headfirst down a stairwell. Not a long stairwell, only a dozen or so steps in it. He clean broke his neck and died right there at the bottom.

Imagine a fall down eighty-four stairs.

The scent of malt drifted up from the brewery as I set about my task. Occasional trains rolled and clattered by below and I prayed that you would not be on any of them, that somehow I had missed you, or that you had changed your routine on the one night I wanted you to stay exactly the same as you always were.

The clock on the SGIO building said 8:03pm by the time it was all set up. I concealed myself behind thick bushes at the top of the stairs. By my feet was the mallet that drove a wooden stake tight into the garden bed opposite. The wire lay loose along the top step, winding like a snake from the stake in the ground to the one in my hand.

I waited, breathing in the malted, muggy air.

◆

'Johnno himself specified that this passage was to be read as we commit him to the earth. He did not give his reasons for this selection; however, perhaps it is fitting that Johnno identified with Christ's plea to His Father in the Garden of Gethsemane.'

This priest had never met you, and here he was calling you Johnno? I closed my eyes tight, trying to shut his voice out.

'Jesus knew his fate. Persecuted by the authorities and betrayed by those He most trusted, this is the voice of the Lord's humanity: Let this cup pass.

'Some may find his choice intriguing. Why would a man like John Calvin Hope, a hero and pillar of the community, choose this reading? It is possible that Johnno, too, may have bargained for more time. Most of us will. Johnno was a brave man, a dedicated police officer with well over twenty years' service in the public good. He made a great many friends throughout the force and the high regard of his colleagues culminated in his award of the Queen's Police Medal. He faced the challenges of upholding law with integrity and bravery. Many of his fellow officers here today would echo that assertion. But Johnno was still a mortal man of dust.

I prefer to think that John's Gospel was an assurance: that even in the darkest hours contemplating his mortality, Johnno, like all of God's children, would not be abandoned. He would not be forsaken.'

I briefy wondered if you even knew the meaning of the word 'contemplation' before the priest's words atomised into nothing. It occurred to me that I couldn't feel my legs. I wanted to ask why no one had provided chairs for the service. I wondered if I should just be done with it and throw myself onto the casket, save the expense of two funerals. I smiled at the thought you could have had a woman on top of you for all eternity.

There were others there. Probably around thirty. A few maybe felt they had to be there out of some sense of duty, people you hadn't driven away altogether. Most of them would have never seen you for who you really were, people under the impression that you were a good bloke. A couple of the old cronies were there, the ones who weren't in hiding or in prison. They were stiff as boards and had the faces of tired, pained men, well beyond their years, each one dressed in their mourning black, their poker-machine faces sagging, melting into puffed-out chests.

I couldn't stop my right hand, the one holding the wire, from shaking. Three people had passed so far, but still there was no sign of you. Three times I drew the wire across the top landing, holding it tight despite both tremor and escalating stiffness in the rest of my body. Each time I realised it wasn't you, I let the wire go and curled back into a tight crouch, not daring to breathe until certain I was alone again. Three times I wondered what on earth had possessed me to do this.

No, Enid. Focus.

The temperature dropped; dew formed on the garden and settled into my skin. My heart pounded in my ears and behind my eyes. In my mind I ran through it again and again, practiced tightening the wire, drawing the wooden stake towards me with slow, angry precision.

Voices.

Panicked, I yanked the wire with a flick of my wrist, unaware a loop had curled around my index finger. It bit down hard, breaking the skin. I whimpered, desperately trying to stifle my voice.

'These are such pissy fuckin' sums! What are you doin' with the rest of it?' said a gruff voice.

'What you want me to do? There's fuck all left after consorting have stuffed their paws into it.' It was your voice of course, but you sounded like someone else entirely. Someone pleading, desperate.

'You're a terrible fuckin' liar, Johnno. Worse than one of my second-tier girls. I know there's more in the pool and I know you've got access to it. Right?'

'Mike, I swear it's the truth. Some of the businesses have been defaulting on payments. We're shaking 'em down, but we still won't see anything for a month or so.'

A tense pause, shuffled feet.

'I'm not going to kill you, Johnno, because you've been good to me in the past. But make no fuckin' mistake. You're gonna have to work harder from now on. My cut's going up fifty per cent.'

At this you fell to your knees. You actually went down on your knees!

'Oh please don't do that! Mike, mate, I can't find another fifty. Oh, Jesus, it'll start eating into my own salary! I could make it up to you some other way.'

I have no memory of you ever saying the word 'please' until then, not even at your most contrite.

Mike seemed to consider your request a moment before responding.

'There is a job that needs doing. A bit of roughing, nothing fancy.'

'Anything, mate.'

'A rabbit on the south side needs to be put back in her place.'

Rabbit?

'Aw jeez, Mike. A woman?'

'You got a problem with that, Johnno?' A pointed, accusatory tone.

Even in my state, I had to agree. You had a problem with that, Johnno?

A pulsing throb behind my eyes. Two people? If I went ahead with the plan, it would change everything. But what of the risks? What if it didn't work? My mouth felt dry and my legs were loose and warm. I grew dizzy. I couldn't catch my breath. My mind fogged, crowded with thoughts, and for one mad second considered running out from my hiding place to warn you.

'*What the fuck are you doin' here?*'

I blinked a few times quickly and exhaled slowly to clear the distraction from my mind.

You remained on your knees, though you were now hunched over, and I could just make out through the bushes you coughing hard and pounding at your chest. Maybe divine intervention would deliver a heart attack.

No.

A hack dislodged whatever had been choking you. With renewed vigour and the pulse behind my eyes sharpening into focus, I steadied my hand and drew the wire taut again. You spat on the footpath and finally answered:

'Nah. I guess not, Mike.'

'Good man. I'll give you the details tomorrow.'

'No worries,' you said, rising back to your feet. 'I gotta go, get home to the fuckin' wench.'

The man laughed breezily. 'I'm down the carpark on Wickham, you want a lift?'

No.

I concentrated on your round, red face, your thick hairy fists. I could still feel that gun jammed to my temple. Focus, Enid. I would not be diverted from my path and neither would you.

'Nah. I'm gonna catch the train.'

'Suit yourself.'

While your companion continued down the footpath towards the carpark, you turned back towards Jacob's Ladder. I tightened my grip further. You could've played that wire like a guitar string.

Three steps, two steps, one step. The wire was set to strike you just above the ankle and you hit at more or less full downhill stride.

'Fu—!'

You couldn't even get the word out as you took a dive down the first flight of stairs, ripping the stake out from my grasp and dragging it after you. You landed face first with a guttural blow, sliding across the concrete and coming to a stop at the second flight. I don't know why, but I pictured you would roll down the length of the staircase until you hit Turbot Street. I guess it came from old cartoons or something.

'Johnno? Was that you mate?' Mike re-emerged. The noise had obviously brought him running back up the street and he stood, sweaty and breathing heavily,

at the top of the stairs where I could see him clearly.
Portly, ruddy, thick moustache, hair slicked back the
same way you did yours. All of you were cut from
the same raw material, weren't you? He descended
to where you lay and picked up the stake I had been
holding, wire still attached.

'Mayck?' Your voice was a slushed, damaged mess.
Still face down, you tried to prop yourself up by the
elbows.

He dropped the stake and stepped backwards.

'Whass goan own?'

'Oh shit,' he muttered. His eyes darted frantically.
At one point he stared directly at the bushes where I
hid, narrowing his eyes for second. Nothing. Within
a minute he was gone, tearing as fast as his potbelly
allowed, I assume towards the safety of his car.

For the next few hours, I waited. Not a soul passed
by; a sleepy city on a nondescript weeknight. It was not
until the SGIO clock read 11:53 that my swollen knees
told me I had waited long enough.

I stood over you, tentatively at first, the mallet in my
hand. I had brought it only as a means of securing the
stakes, but as I waited, I had regarded with growing

fascination its dull, rubber head. It was inarticulate, brute: a man's instrument, both tool and weapon.

You had half rolled onto your side, the result of having tried so many times to push yourself up from the concrete. Even in the darkness, I could see your palms grazed, your face a messed mash of blood, tissue and gravel.

I took a deep, unsteady breath and gripped the mallet's handle tighter. I didn't even look around for a final check to ensure we were still alone. I raised it aloft. Years of terror and brutality had hardened me in ways I never imagined possible. My energy and resolve crystallised into a single act of terrible violence. Even before the first blow I felt an overwhelming sense of elation. Relief. I was in control. I needed to do this. And without blinking I let myself loose.

One. *Holy Mary,*

Two. *Mother of God.*

Three. *Pray for us sinners.*

Four. *Now, and at the*

Five. *hour of our death.*

I wiped my face with a handkerchief, staining red what had been clean white linen. I placed the mallet—

pasted with blood and hair—into my handbag and stepped over your body to continue down the stairs. With a little luck, I thought, I might catch the last train home.

Empty words and a small pile of dirt through the air and down on your coffin, deep in the earth where you were to remain.

The stone lay nearby, ready to be set over your head. It took me a long time to put those words together. Beneath the badge of the police force (*Firmness with Courtesy*):

John Calvin Hope, 1929 – 1989. Loving husband, provider, missed by all.

Outrageous lies, but what else could I say?

Crooked cop, wife beater, I hope you rot in hell.

Ever since I cracked your head open, lies had replaced routine as my protective armour.

My mind raced through all the things I had planned to do when you died. I could travel, meet new people, make a fresh beginning as though you had never happened to me. But I hadn't counted on the twin effects of advancing years and a meagre income. How much freedom could I really look forward to?

I pictured my own epitaph:

Here lies Enid Grace Hope. She stayed with him twenty-seven years. Three out of love, sixteen out of fear, and eight out of guilt.

Did you manage to take away the last of my independence by dying?

❦

It had all the unintentional comedy of a bad American police drama: you sat propped up by a tower of pillows, your doctor stood at the end of the bed, to your right the Assistant Commissioner in full uniform, and to the left your loving wife.

You had the doctor fooled well enough. She thought you were 'good value', a real charmer. Two weeks out of a months-long coma. Recovering, but not out of the woods. Most of the damage was to what they called the occipital and parietal lobes of the brain. It wasn't quite enough to kill you, but your vision was blotchy and you would need a wheelchair for the rest of your life.

You coped well with this news, so well the doctors at first worried that you weren't really with it. Those jokes about nicknaming yourself 'Hot Wheels' were a bit much. Eventually they shrugged and figured you were happy enough to have survived such a brutal attack. I knew better. The sidelong glances at me when no one else was watching told me so. You were storing the hate, the fear, the sickness. Nothing had changed.

'Well Mrs Hope, your husband is doing very well. He should be able to come home very soon.'

'What do you think of that *honeybunch*?'

'Oh, lovely,' I said to my hands before looking back up to the doctor's triumphant face.

'She's a good woman, doc. Great cook you know. All the good stuff, shepherd's pie, steak and chips.'

'Not too much of that fatty food, Johnno,' said the doctor with mock finger shaking.

You laughed and turned your attention back to me. 'A good woman,' you continued, 'but she'll be the death of me.'

Your smile never faltered for a second.

The doctor made her way out and the Assistant Commissioner cleared his throat politely. You and I both turned to him obediently.

'I'm very happy to hear you are well on your way, John.'

'Thanks, boss.'

He offered us a pained smile. 'If there's anything that we can do for you, just let us know. As far as we are concerned, you were injured in the line of duty.'

'Jeez, everyone has been so good to me, what with buying the wheelchair and all.'

'It's the least we can do. But, John, I'm here on more official business.'

You narrowed your eyes.

'I've spoken at length to the Commissioner and he has agreed to recommend you for the Queen's Police Medal. Congratulations!'

Eyes wide again, you scratched your forehead in wonder. The wound where the wire broke the skin on my finger throbbed.

Clearly uncomfortable with silence, the Assistant Commissioner continued, 'Given the suspicious circumstances of your...accident and your tireless work in the CIB, we are granting the medal for services in the public interest fighting organised crime in the city.'

'This…' you choked. Were you going to cry? 'This is the happiest day of my life.'

My smile hardened.

I know you used to do it on purpose. I watched you one day, looking out through the kitchen curtains. You pushed your wheelchair through the back door and along the concrete path that stretched into the garden, between the birds of paradise where you would be better concealed. There, surrounded by floral beaks you would violently push the chair sideways, throwing your body over the armrests and down into the dirt below.

'Enid? *Enid!*'

On cue I would rush out. 'Honey, what happened?'

'You stupid bitch! When are you going to fix this path? And this cheap chair falls apart the second I breathe on it the wrong way! Those crooks who bought it are getting exactly what's coming to them!'

When a Royal Commission into police corruption was announced, I waited for the truth to emerge. But as the people drawn into scandal rose higher and higher to include the Commissioner, various Ministers, and finally the Premier himself, I gave up any notion that I might see John Hope's name sullied in a news report. You were forgotten: a disabled has-been, a small-time thug in a vast ocean of crime and corruption.

'There's nothing wrong with the chair. Let me help you up, dear.'

'I don't need your help! I hope Fitzgerald hangs them up by their balls! Fuckin' Queen's Medal! Where's the rest of my fuckin' pension? They called me a hero! A *hero*!'

We discovered soon after your 'accident' how little you had earned in superannuation over your thirty-odd years of service. Within a year we were reduced to getting by on a standard pension.

The early mornings were just as quiet as they had always been, but I no longer plotted my escape.

I righted your chair and lifted you back into it.

'There you go, we must do something about that path, hey?'

'Where are you going? I haven't finished with you!'

❧

The last of the mourners faded into the sunlight. No one approached me, not even the priest. I was left standing next to the open hole. That's when I finally began to cry.

I wanted to curse you again and again, curse that it took you eight years to die. Eight years of pushing you in the wheelchair, helping you move to the bed, to the bath, to the toilet. Spending every waking minute with you, carrying the increasingly heavy knowledge that I was the one who put you in that chair. I covered my face and moaned into my hands, sinking to my knees like you had done that night at the top of Jacob's Ladder.

I wanted to scream. I wanted everyone in the world to know that I hated you with every fibre of my being and yet I stayed. I wanted to dump this unbearable, crushing guilt into your grave with you. But I knew I wouldn't rid myself of it that easily.

The tears flowed until I was too exhausted to continue.

Eventually, I took from my handbag the string of rosary beads that had been a wedding gift from my mother. I turned them over in my hand, the jasper stone blood red in the afternoon sun. I had turned to them more times than I remember during our marriage. Now, I wondered what possible use I would have for a pointless talisman. I broke the string and threw the beads with as much force as I could muster. They hit the lid of your casket with satisfying machine-gun cracks.

I wondered briefly what I would do with the rest of the day.

Frangipani

She waited at the edge of the verandah, a glass of water as always by her feet. From under broken and rusted blinds, she watched the street and waited. Adeline had already waited so long. When she moved here with her husband, the house was glorious, propped up by low hardwood stumps on thirty-two perches. Then, it was a house full of promise. Now, paint peeled from the weatherboards. The windows had acquired a patina of grime, almost opaque. Dotted throughout the front yard were the dead remains of what had once been a grove of frangipanis.

Stabs of lightning threw alarming shadows on the floor and Adeline saw the outline of herself, an old woman jitterbugging across the cracked and silvery boards. The storm was not far now. With a shaky hand, she sipped her water. Anxiety had formed a dense knot in her abdomen, a familiar feeling that had little to do with the weather.

The wireless played a crackly ABC theme and an announcer reminded her it was January 25, 1974. Adeline closed her eyes and nodded silently. Katie had been gone twelve years, one month, and thirteen days. The dull pain that always accompanied a tally throbbed in her head in time with the lightning strikes and radio static. She vaguely registered the increasingly alarming warnings and news of a cyclone called 'Wanda' before she switched the wireless off altogether. She didn't need any more voices.

'Mrs Jolley?'

So clear, the doctor's voice, soft and hesitant.

)

'Mrs Jolley? Mr Jolley? I think there's a problem with your daughter.'

Adeline lay back in the hospital bed, sweating. Joseph smiled through cigar smoke. Right from first sight, Katie simply didn't look right. Large head. Eyes wide apart, flat nose. They took her away from her mother after only the briefest time together. Some called her 'mongoloid', others called it 'down syndrome' as though a change of name would make a difference.

'There are many good homes available for girls with her needs.'

Joseph stared at his shoes and put the cigar out.

'Katie already has a good home,' Adeline said evenly.

'She will not have a normal child's mental capacity. She will need care beyond what you can provide for her,' the doctor grunted.

'You think we can't look after our own daughter?'

Joseph plunged his hands into his pockets and said nothing. He always avoided conflict. The doctor sighed, muttered something about giving them time. He spun on his heels and left.

'What if he's right?' said Joseph.

Adeline frowned.

'What if something happens to Katie? What if we can't look after her?'

She took her husband's hand. 'We'll do whatever we have to.'

The doctor called again, this time from the hall outside.

'Mrs Jolley!'

'Mrs Jolley!'

Adeline blinked the doctor away and peered over the handrail. Her neighbour stood waving his arms at the front gate, wearing galoshes and a yellow plastic raincoat.

Drawing as much energy as she could muster, Adeline raised her voice. 'Yes dear?' she said.

'Mrs Jolley, we've got to get out of here. The bank has already broken. They're evacuating this whole area.'

'I'll be along soon.'

The neighbour hesitated. 'Do you need a hand?'

'No, dear, I'll be fine.'

If there was one thing Adeline could do, it was manage on her own. *There's no one to help. You'll have to look after her all on your own. Joseph has to work to put food on the table. He has to travel. Those sales don't happen by magic.*

'You can't stay waiting out here for...' he paused and shuffled his feet. 'You can't stay. Please, I'll help you.'

'No. Thank you for letting me know. I'll be along very shortly. Please don't come in.'

The neighbour opened the gate. A thunderclap underscored the squeak and groan of the gate's hinges. Adeline's eyes opened wild. How dare he presume to take her away from her own house! How dare he tell her that Katie would never pass a mental age of four! What is 'mental age' supposed to mean anyway? Low claps and grumbles from the sodden sky reverberated through her chest and bubbled up to her throat. Adeline scrambled for something that might keep this man out of her yard. She picked up a handful of stones from a pot plant and threw them with a venom that surprised even her.

'Ow! Hey, what are you doing?'

She replied with another handful. Stones and soil sprayed the front fence and one or two larger projectiles hit target. Adeline picked up a third handful of mostly soil and drew her fist back, waiting for the next throw, staring down the intruder.

'Hey! Shit, I'm trying to help you, you crazy old goat!'

Adeline said nothing; she simply held the ammunition in place and stood her ground. Her message was clear: disturb the protective mother at your own risk.

'Fine. You want to fucking drown, that's on you.' On his way out he stopped and turned back. 'It doesn't matter how long you wait here for her, Mrs Jolley. She's never coming back.'

Adeline did not listen. She settled back in her chair and watched up and down the street. She took a sip of water. Crickets struck up a call and response—

phhhtch! phhhtch! phhhtch!

—a continuation of the same conversation that began when Katie played under the frangipanis in the front yard.

⸙

After no more than a minute (*no more than a minute you must believe me*), she looked up from the Christmas cards she had been writing. Her daughter had been playing happily, darting between the trees, laughing and singing songs to herself. Now she was gone. Adeline stood and leaned over the railing.

'Katie?'

Nothing but crickets.

phhhtch! phhhtch! phhhtch!

Adeline hurtled down the stairs and dashed between gnarled trunks and branches. She found no one. Why would Katie go quiet so suddenly?

'Katie!'

phhhtch! phhhtch! phhhtch!

She checked the sides of the house, breathing hard. Sweating. She returned to the house, to anywhere Katie might have hidden inside, then out the back. She bolted back and forth between fences, screaming across the neighbours' yards.

'KATIE!'

Her chest heaved as she wandered the neighbourhood, the shops, along the main road. She flailed aimlessly through a sea of unfamiliar faces, of cars and trams, of dark shadows crawling across the road. Panic gave way to terror; curious faces dissolved into a blur of tears.

Finally, she collapsed onto the footpath, a damp, irregular mass. Panic and grief infused her body and leached out onto the earth. She made attempts to continue searching, dragging her body over the earth. Every breath in was an ugly gulp of wretched, foul air. Her voice had become little more than a brutal croak.

Did she lose consciousness? Adeline was never sure. Someone must have pitied her eventually, taken her home, telephoned Joseph, alerted the authorities, set the next decade in motion. But none of it made the slightest difference.

Katie was gone.

⟩

The first drops hit the tin roof, loud as hail. The sky at last opened up and dumped teeming fat rain on the earth. Adeline took a sip from her glass. Katie was gone. And everyone already had the whole story figured out in their heads.

⟩

The police arrived, interviewed Adeline, picked around the house without much interest. They interviewed Joseph, established that he was out of town on a last-minute business trip. They interviewed him again. And again.

Everyone knew. When Adeline entered a room, people stopped talking. When she left a room, whispers followed her.

Something wasn't right. Little handicapped girls don't just go missing.

Not like that.

’

Adeline heard the crash even through the white noise of rain on tin. Rough, careless footfall from the bathroom. Despite the clatter of natural destruction outside, she stepped carefully across the verandah to the front door, taking care to avoid the squeaky floorboards. More noise from inside the house. Her hands shook, spilling water over her fingers. Adeline stared at the glass for a moment; she'd forgotten she was still holding it.

'Hey Maaaaaahhhhhmm?'

A cold jolt. The glass slipped from her hand and smashed on the floor. Dizzy, Adeline reached out to steady herself but only brushed the wall. She fell to her hands and knees. The heel of her palm landed squarely on jagged shards, razor sharp. It sliced through her wrist so cleanly she did not immediately feel anything. She raised her arm, stared at the bloodied glass embedded. With deep breath, she braced herself and yanked one of the larger pieces out. Pain flowered through her. She reeled and slumped back against the wall.

Another noise, much closer now. Footsteps. Definitely. Footsteps approaching.

'Mum?'

Adeline stared back. She could not speak; she could barely breathe. Her wrist throbbed. She held it tight to slow the flow of blood, but steady pulses dripped onto the floor. Tiny explosions of ruby red in a field of diamonds.

'Mum, you're hurt.'

Adeline blinked through tears and shivered. Katherine Barbara Jolley stood before her, exactly as she remembered, slouching a little in her orange summer playsuit. Frilly socks poked out from black patent leather shoes, heavily scuffed on the inside where she dragged her feet. She was perfect, exactly as she was in Adeline's dreams. Twelve years, one month, and thirteen days. The ache of the tally receded, but in its place was an overwhelming tangle of confusion and fear.

Katie turned her nose up a little. 'I hate blood.'

Adeline sat up. A savage gust of wind blew the front

door open and rain spattered through. Without a word, Katie lifted her mother by the elbow and together they shuffled to the bathroom. Katie washed the blood off and tried to rub a towel across the wound, but jumped away in fright when Adeline cried out in pain. Adeline took the towel and tied it into a makeshift covering. When she finally spoke, Adeline's voice was small and bewildered.

'I love you.'

Katie caught her mother's eye and replied with a self-conscious smile.

'Awwwww, Mum!'

Without any guidance, Katie plucked another towel and wrapped it around the one already on Adeline's wrist. She held it with both hands. Adeline had taught her this. Years before, when Katie fell off her bike, Adeline showed her how to apply pressure to stop bleeding. Katie may not have learned how to tie a knot, but she knew exactly what needed to be done. She was not stupid.

A long creaking groan emerged from under the floorboards, the sound of an old ship on the high seas. With her free hand, Adeline touched her daughter's hair, her face, her shoulders and arms. Katie was not a phantom; she was real. She had returned to her mother.

'Where's your father, Katie? Is he still away? He should be here with us.'

They were hardly subtle about it. When the police spoke to Joseph a fourth time, they handcuffed him and took him into the station. The cuffs were for no one's protection. They paraded Joseph out the front door, across the verandah, down the front steps and into the waiting car at the front. Adeline screamed at them, called them lazy bastards, ordered them to stop terrorising her husband and start looking for their daughter. The ruckus brought everyone from the neighbourhood out into their yards. The nosy bitch from number forty-three nodded her approval and called out:

'About bloody time!'

Joseph stayed in the watch house that night. He never told Adeline much about what happened there, what questions they asked, why they suspected him at all, why he walked gingerly in the weeks that followed.

But even if they had good reason for taking Joseph in, they still let him go. One of the younger constables openly told Adeline they couldn't make the charges against Joseph 'stick', like it was shit on a clean white wall. But while nothing stuck in the watch house, back in the neighbourhood Joseph could never cleanse his name. There was a betting pool on where he'd hidden Katie's body. Most of the money was on him dumping her in the river past the ferry stop at the end of street. He was refused service in the shops. His existence was not acknowledged at the bank. People avoided passing him on footpaths.

But if the consensus on Joseph assumed his guilt, the community was divided on Adeline.

The poor darling, how could she live with him knowing what he did?

Or do you think she knew about it?

She must have known something was going on, don't you think?

How could she not?

Joseph's employer asked him to move out of sales and into a lower-paid desk job. Eventually, like their friends who faded away, his work trickled down to nothing.

Joseph was never sacked from the firm, he was simply starved of commission, surrounded by people hostile, frightened, or pitying.

The first thing Joseph did after he left the job was cut down all the frangipanis in the front yard, the trees Katie loved to play under. With the view unobstructed, he pulled up a seat on the verandah where he would stay for years to come. Adeline busied herself with posting photographs and taking out newspaper advertisements seeking information on Katie's true abductor. They didn't go out much, Joseph especially. Any hope that the whispers would peter out over time proved hopelessly optimistic. The longer Katie remained missing, the stronger the whispers grew until Joseph's name was spoken in past tense, even if he was in earshot.

When they fished him out of the river, floating face down and drifting out towards the bay, the gossips and the cops considered the case closed. It must have been the guilt, gnawing away at him until he couldn't take any more.

Must have been.

And, for Adeline, Katie was never further away.

The creaking grew louder under their feet, hardening into alarming thumps and cracks. Ugly, filthy water loaded with organic detritus flowed in through the bathroom door and up through the floor waste, swirling around the tiny room as it rose. Adeline stood and considered what they might do from here.

'We need to leave,' she said, more to herself than to her daughter.

Katie raised her arms. Adeline smiled and lifted her daughter up on the side of her uninjured hand. How light she felt, Adeline thought, how effortless to carry her. Katie nestled into her neck and whispered, 'I'm scared.'

'You have nothing to worry about, darling. Mum is here now.'

Adeline pushed through the rising, quickening current, heading for the front yard and the street beyond. The towel—now completely darkened with blood—loosened but she had no time to secure it again. A layer of mud and silt was thickening on the floor. Adeline lost first one shoe, then the other. Progress was slow. Before long she realised it was easier to stop trying to walk, cling more tightly to Katie, and let the water carry them wherever it wanted. Neither of them had learned to swim and Adeline slapped at the surface of the water in a feeble effort to appear in control. They floated swiftly through the kitchen to the back door. Adeline pushed against the top of the doorframe to stop them hitting it.

'Katie?'

'Yes?'

'How long can you hold your breath?'

'I don't know.'

Plastic bowls and cups had lifted out of the overhead cupboards and they circled in a gurgling, bubbling brown whirlpool just in front of the doorframe.

'Let's play a game.'

'Okay.'

'When I count to three you take a big breath and you hold it as long as you can, okay?'

'Okay.'

The water stung Adeline's eyes as she peered through swirling silt. The current dragged them down to the sludge, shoved them against the screen door.

Katie clung tighter to her side, her eyes shut tight, her cheeks puffed out. Adeline kicked at the door, opening a hole through the flyscreen. A rush of cold water welled through the threshold before pulling them through. They tumbled out in to the yard, dodging the objects of Adeline's life—bedding, radio, books, furniture—as they jostled with felled trees, shorn away lengths of weatherboard, a whole car body. Adeline felt Katie's hands loosen and release; she thrashed around after her, desperate flailing, kicking. The water darkened, clouds of blood. Adeline no longer knew which way was up. Her wrist ached, her arms and legs grew weary. She rubbed at her eyes. The temptation to take a breath, to let the water flow into her lungs, was unbearable. Grief descended again over her, smothered and muzzled her. For a moment, no more than a snapshot in time, she had been relieved of its pall and dared to imagine the change was permanent. But Katie had again been snatched away and Adeline resigned herself to the lonely and bitter end she always knew would be her lot. She opened her eyes, determined to remain conscious as the darkness claimed her.

A single flower tumbled by, the thick yellow and white petals of a frangipani. A well of warmth rose from below, cushioned, and carried her to calmer, lighter waters. Another frangipani and another and another swirled on the eddies around her. Summoning one last scrap of energy, she reached out to the flowers, but her hands found nothing but more water. A familiar landmark passed below: the ferry stop that had separated street from river. Adeline hugged herself. She would not be lonely for much longer. She felt no fear. Cocooned in warm, floral floodwater, Adeline could happily jitterbug down the river and right into the bay.

The vague embrace of water solidified: she felt an arm across her back and another under her legs. Adeline blinked and squinted up to see who was escorting her. A face silhouetted against a halo of impossibly bright sunlight. It was a young woman's face, round cheeks and chin, long hair tied back. A voice, like the voices that once echoed in Adeline's head, now filled her heart.

'I'm sorry I lost you.'

'You lost me?'

'It doesn't matter now. Dad's waiting for us.'

Adeline smiled as they danced through the flotsam

of a life left behind. Ahead of her lay something unknowable, but wonderful. It was just out there with Joseph, drifting somewhere in the bay. And her daughter was taking her to it. She wanted to nestle into Katie's arms, but she found herself curling into nothing but water and flowers. For now she would have to wait.

That was alright. Adeline was used to waiting.

Coda

Am I awake?

There's a clock in here somewhere—its incessant ticking sometimes resonates through me—but it's never been in my line of sight. Time itself has become elasticised: days, hours, and minutes warp and distort my reality. I never realised that soul-crushing boredom could coexist so comfortably with desperate urgency, but here we are. The worst of all possible apocalypses. Despite appearances, this is not a hospital, not exactly. Palliative care is a place to be made comfortable, to wait it out. Nevertheless, I am woken (*woken?*) at regular intervals to the schedule of healthcare systems: medication, turns, machine checks, transfers. Check my name, my date of birth. Bed to chair. Chair to bed. Sometimes a chat, though not often. I'm not a great conversationalist.

Early on, I was given the brief. I cannot talk. I cannot move my arms. I cannot nod or shake my head. All my communication must now happen in binary.

eyes up—*yes*

eyes down—*no*

They only move vertically, my eyes I mean; I can't even look at anyone sidelong. So my conversations tend to happen within, an internal monologue reverberating in half-lit emptiness, a feedback loop with no volume control. Through this, I must document what I understand, interrogate it, commit it to memory.

I have seen myself, a mirror held out before me. My outward appearance is someone I cannot recognise: his twisted face waxy red, a body wired, ventilated, augmented. I am kept alive by the machines attached to me, the people that complement them, the systems that brought it all together. Does that make me some kind of human-machine hybrid? I am a cybernetic organism; a technological marvel whose only power is to generate conscious thoughts I cannot express.

Since the coma, I live mostly between worlds. The ghost of cold grey light fills the space around me, never quite illuminating anything. It leaks in from the corridors outside my room, into my sleep, into my dreams. I drift seamlessly between states of existence, never quite locating myself, grasping at moments, memories, ideas. In my dreams I could be anywhere, with anyone, doing whatever my unconscious mind can conjure. I could fly. Instead, it's more of the same. I feel cheated.

A sudden jolt stirs me. Something is happening. A nurse turns the overhead lights on and raises the blinds, letting in a modicum of filtered sunlight.

'Good morning, Martin!'

I blink.

'Did you want something?'

—*no*

'Your wife is coming soon, Martin. Won't that be exciting?'

—*yes*

◆

When I see her, I am again astonished at my reaction. The effortless grace with which she moves, the simple gratification of a smile directed at me. Galina is so beautiful, I am overwhelmed, tears roll down my cheeks. Fortunately, she is too distracted to notice. She is not alone.

'Dad!'

They launch onto my chair, sending it rocking backwards. They wrap their arms around my neck and compete with each other to tell me whatever is on their minds, words bursting out at a rapid clip left and right.

'...and then Damian was like noooo way so we tried a longer ramp and set it up at the back...'

'...it wasn't like the show on TV and Mum bought me a violin but I want a cello like hers...'

'Kids! Stop hanging off your father, you're going to hurt him!'

Conrad leaps from the chair and turns his attention to the ventilator, inspecting its castors, sorely tempted I'm sure to press a few buttons. Shelley is more reluctant, she frees her arms but her fingers cling to my shirt like cobblers pegs.

'I'm not finished!' she cries.

Galina grabs our daughter first at the hips, then the ankles, attempting to drag her away from me.

'Shelley! Let go! You're making your father cough!'

I'm not coughing, Gala. I'm laughing! I'm laughing!

The children are dispatched to the common room where I hear the television flicked over to cartoons.

'I'm sorry.'

—no

She lifts my hand off its support, allows it to curl around hers. I ache for the memory of that feeling. Gala is as beautiful as ever, but up close I see she is flagging, a long way from the woman who so recently made her solo debut on the Concert Hall platform. Her shoulders slump, her eyes blink slowly. Her breaths are uneven and her mouth is set, teeth clenched. She is actively stopping herself from crying. She withdraws from me for a moment, vanishing from my field of vision. When she returns, she is again smiling. I want to smile back.

'Do you want to go outside?'

With you? More than anything.

—*yes*

'Good. We...we should talk.'

Talk? That's a statement that lingers in my memory. Haven't we been here before?

I am reasonably portable. The machines I cannot live without can be attached to my chair and run on battery power for a short time. I form a cumbersome, hulking mass of equipment, but she manages to manoeuvre me well enough out the corridor, through the common room doors and into the garden. The world outside floods my senses, the fragrance of frangipani in the still humid air. I want to take a deep breath, absorb everything.

Gala positions me under the shade of a palm, careful to keep me out of direct sunlight. In a distant corner of the garden, a few smokers form a huddle and mumble to each other.

She throws herself down on the bench beside me and sighs, staring at the ground.

I want to tell her I'm sorry.

We've been here before. The memory of her nervous pacing interrupting my work. I was irritable already. I remember that. She told me then: *We need to talk.* Fine, okay. What do you want? When she looked back at me, her nervousness dissolved into concern.

Martin, are you okay?

I don't have any memory after that.

I wish I could shrug. The therapist is nice enough I guess, a little chirpy. Is she a speech therapist or occupational therapist? What's even the difference?

'This is only temporary,' she assures me. 'We'll mount them onto board once you choose the ones you prefer.'

A small stack of rough photocopies on large sheets of paper, propped up on a music stand. The first page is a random grid of 'feeling words' augmented by simple icons: WHAT, WHEN, WHERE, COME, HURT, GIVE, LISTEN, HAPPY, SAD, TIRED, ANGRY, OK, LOVE, HELP, PLAY. There's no real pattern I can discern. Emotionally, it's all over the place.

She demonstrates how it works, runs her pen vertically until I indicate the correct line, then horizontally until I choose a tile.

'You understand?'

—*yes*

'What do you think of this board?'

Fine. I mean, it's a little limited, but I get what's happening. I'm being offered an outlet. I indicate a tile on the board.

OK

'Just okay?'

—*yes*

'Let's try another.'

She swaps out the icons for letters. I try to remember the points for each of them as scrabble tiles. Getting closer here, except the letters are in a strange order. I stare at them for a while, tuning the therapist's twittering out, wrapping my head around the code embedded in the order.

E T A I N O S H R D L U C M F W Y G P B V K Q J X Z

Frequency? It looks like frequency. Makes sense I suppose, but it's an unholy mess arranged in a grid like this.

'What do you think?'

—*no*

The next is a much more familiar arrangement. I accept it makes no more sense than the last one, but seeing those letters in that order is like arriving home after an odyssey through the wilderness. She can see it in my eyes before I've indicated either —*yes* or —*no*.

'I wondered if this might be more your style.'

That's just the problem, Martin. It's your style.

Not just a return home. It's a lure into the past, a memory from before that insists on encroaching my present reality. Jane, my agent, sitting across the table from me, on her second glass of pinot gris, her block hand gestures underscoring the cold hard truths she lays between us.

I've tried, Martin. I really have, but it's a little too bold a little too out there. All that momentum from the first two novels. It all just kind of crashed with the last one and I'd be lying if I said that wasn't factoring into this. It's a cruel business I know. But this manuscript, it's just not what anyone is looking for from Martin Venn. If it were up to me, I'd publish it in a heartbeat, but you know how things are. It might have gotten up a few years ago with a boutique outfit, but in this economic climate everyone is tightening their schedules, looking for sure things. The decisions are all so conservative, no one is taking any risks. It pisses me off, to be frank. There are plenty of times I want to pack it all in. Have you thought about doing memoir?

The therapist runs her pen over the board and I indicate the first row.

Qu W E R T Y U I O P

That 'Qu' is a nice touch. So too the additional non-keyboard tiles: START, STOP, MISTAKE, CHANGE BOARD.

I indicate a letter.

P

That lunch with Jane was my last. I left with no agent, no prospects, and a split bill. She hasn't come to see me here. I doubt she would even know.

E

With each new pass on the board, we pick up a little speed.

R

The letters begin to flow.

F

I am struck by the beautiful economy of the language.

E

It's all there in those three rows: the entire corpus.

C

And everything yet to come.

T

All I have to do is put those letters in the right order.

◆

The neurologist looks over her glasses at me, her eyes bright and intense.

'This is good news, Martin. The infection has stabilised and we need to think now about what the next steps should be.'

Next steps? I can't see her, but beside me, Gala sighs. I want to squeeze her hand, a tiny act of solidarity and apology.

This doctor I'm told has been with me from the beginning, since I was transferred from emergency. I've been assured she is one of the best. It bothers me that I cannot remember the names of any of these people here, the people who care for me and keep me alive. It must have been her who first explained what had happened and what that meant for me, though I don't remember acquiring this knowledge at all.

I had a cerebrovascular accident, a haemorrhage from a blood vessel into my brain, the leaked blood effectively killing the function of anything it touched. In my case it touched a highly specific part of the brainstem. They must have shown me diagrams from an anatomy textbook because my mental picture is clear. First locate the stem that connects the mush of cortex to the spinal cord. At the centre of that stem you will find the ventral pons, a node of neurological fibres sandwiched between the midbrain and medulla oblongata.

Got all that? Good.

I've seen people with strokes before: they might lose movement on one side of their body or sometimes the ability to speak. A few can even recover back to full function. Me? I lost all voluntary movement and a good chunk of sensation. It's rare, so rare that numbers are hard to come by because the diagnosis is sometimes missed. Lucky me. There is no possibility that I will regain anything I've lost. I will not be able to take in a deep breath, I will not be able to smile.

I have locked in syndrome. Yes, that's what it's called. And to think how much I used to rail against euphemistic language.

Gala's sigh expressed everything I was thinking. What possible next steps could there be?

Wait. They're still talking and I've lost the thread of their conversation. I try to attract someone's attention, blinking furiously.

'...domiciliary care...'

Are they talking about sending me home? How is that even possible? No, not home. A nursing home, of course. My body is stabilised and I am to be moved elsewhere, a place more suitable for a longer wait I suppose.

Still, a tiny shift, a spasm in time, opens up before me. And the communication board beckons.

❧

She stares at her hands. I want to reassure her, tell her that whatever it is on her mind, whatever she has been so hesitant to share, I am capable of receiving. Please, Gala. Unburden yourself.

'I guess this is good news.'

—*yes*

'We'll need to do some research. Find out where there's vacancies. I wonder if you can come and look at places with me.'

I don't know but I say —*yes* anyway.

'We should probably do something about it soon. Things are going to get...tricky before long.'

Tricky. She notices my lack of response either way.

'I have told you. You don't remember, do you?'

—*no*

She holds a weary hand to her head. I have a sinking feeling. Has time played a trick on me? How many times have we had this discussion?

'I'm pregnant, Martin. Again.'

With me?

I try to stitch together a timeline, from stroke, through coma, to my time here. None of it adds up, none of it makes the slightest sense to me.

'I'm well into the second trimester.' She digs through her handbag. 'Dr. Lucy is really happy with our progress. Remember her? The obstetrician?'

—*yes*

I'll admit, that's a lie.

Gala finds the photograph and holds it in front of me. It's an ultrasound scan. There it (*he/she/they*) is: a tiny body in profile, arms up in front of its face.

'We need to find somewhere for you before...'

In that trailed off sentence, we catch a clear glimpse of the difficult road ahead for her. A heavy silence grows between us until Gala suddenly breaks the spell, bursting into tears. I want to comfort her, wrap my arms around her, stroke her hair. I want to tell her everything will be alright. That's not a lie at all. I believe it will.

Dropped by my agent, facing the prospect of having to look for work, something completely alien to me, I dragged myself home, a fucking loser, washed up before my career had a chance to really start. The bitterness lodged in the back of my throat, too large and jagged to swallow. That was my state of mind when she first told me she was pregnant with Conrad. That's not an excuse. She was upset then too and I chose not to comfort her. I couldn't think of worse circumstances under which to bring a child into this world and I let her know. Again and again. I was an arse.

But that was then. That was someone else.

Frustration grips me with such force, I want to explode from this chair. I want my rage to obliterate the cage I'm in, the machines I'm enmeshed with, the pain and guilt that's sitting on my chest and refuses to move. I can't say it enough. The board is right there beside her, propped on its music stand, and still I can't say it. I'm so sorry, Gala. I'm not that man anymore. I mean, just look at me. Look at what I'm saying and understand, please.

—no

'Okay,' she says suddenly. She closes her eyes and resets, steels herself. 'Enough of that.' She lifts her chin ever so slightly and straightens her back into a professional posture. 'We have a lot to do.' She seems to grow, right in front of me. I wish I had a fraction of that strength. God, I love her.

—*yes*

'Mum!' a scream from the common room. 'Shelley hid the remote control and now there's boring stuff on TV!'

Gala brings a hand to her mouth, holding back a smile. 'They're disturbing the other patients, aren't they?'

—*no*

What I mean is: I don't care.

She fetches the children and herds them back into my room, gently explaining that this is a quiet space and there are sick people who need to rest. Shelley spies my communication board, takes it from the stand and lays it on her lap. She pretends to type, watching me to ensure I'm paying attention to her.

Yes, I'm not proud of my behaviour when Gala first told me she was pregnant, but I grew accustomed to the idea of having children, and eventually I welcomed our growing family. I found a job, not great but it paid. Our lives took a different course to the one I had pictured when we were first married. I made a choice and it was the right choice. I didn't write for a long time after that. I felt no need to.

Now our lives have taken another course again.

Here's some free advice. Writer's block? It's a bullshit, pathetic excuse.

◆

Time here repeats itself. Events echo off the grey walls of my memory until they form a dense mesh of noise. It's not something I can actively navigate anymore.

I remember when the future was something I gave little thought to: a vast expanse before me in which I was free to make my own way. Adventure embraced me. Now I have only an acute, urgent present. I might have fluked a transfer out of here and into longer-term accommodation, but it's no more than a brief stay of execution. I'm under no illusion. My future has withered, my plans all speculative.

Enough of useless memories.

Through the fog of waking/dreaming/past/present I must try to find focus. My children who hang off my chair and disturb the peace will barely remember any of this. Prompted maybe by photographs, for them I will be a fuzzy recollection: small details, machines and odours. Soon they will have another sibling, a child for whom I will only be a spectral presence, an unknowable source of regret and sadness: *you look so much like him.*

To the three of you and Gala too: I'm sorry I can't stay.

I might not have a future, but you do. And in this urgent present, I must find a way to reach you there.

When she can, Gala writes these words for me. And when she cannot, I cling to the thread of my thoughts for when we reconvene. I see strings of letters forming words and I move them in my mind with a dexterity I never imagined possible until now. The words form sentences, the sentences paragraphs, the paragraphs lay bare the fragments of a soul desperate to be heard, seen, understood. Of course, all that is nothing new. Is what I write here—indeed, anything I've ever written and recorded—truly representative of me? Will it even last to reach its intended audience?

This is what consumes whatever time I have left.

❧

Last night, Gala stayed late. She lowered the side rail and lay awkwardly beside me. She brought with her a book of poetry. From her lips she conjured the Byzantium of Yeats, a ghost empire that exists only in the rich histories and art that, left in its wake, now burn like coal to be discovered and rediscovered, its immortality assured in pigments, ink, and repetition.

The communication board witnessed this, propped up at the end of the bed.

The letters are all there.

I just have to put them in order.

Author's Note

Many of the stories here have been previously published (though in early and sometimes quite different forms). If you care to look at the dates attached to those publications, you'll realise that *Ephemeral City* is an idea I've been kicking around for more than two decades. In that time, the stories here—conceived as a collective entity—have been split apart, glommed onto a separate narrative, hived off into a short story collection, and generally moved between the foreground and background of my attention. But I never completely left behind that initial idea: the portrait of a city over time revealed through people at the margins, people who passed through, who never expected to be remembered.

It was an idea that struggled to find its best expression until it had attached itself to the parallel notion of using ephemera as a kind of connective tissue, to draw the stories closer together while allowing them the individual space to breathe. As a reader, you are free to approach each story individually or construct them in whatever way you like. You can make connections between them and draw meaning from that, whether it was intentional or not on my part. You can regard the ephemera as essential or as complementary. They're your stories now. I'm ready to let them go. I've held onto them long enough.

Though its roots stretch back, this book is not a retrospective. The first draft of the narrative that would become *Ephemeral City* doesn't exactly make me cringe, but I know why it never quite landed. When I first wrote 'Coda', for example, I was younger than Martin Venn and I was yet to have any children of my own. In that version of the story I did not centre Martin fully and instead contrasted him with another character. In these rapidly advancing years, I felt such sleight of hand was no longer necessary. And, in revisiting him for this book, I had to jettison the entire text of that earlier story and tell it again from scratch. Despite their long gestation, these are stories written *now*: this strange world of doubt and uncertainty in desperate danger of backsliding into something darker and more dangerous.

But these stories, collectively, do not invoke despair. At least that's far from my intention. Like the ephemera that weave their way through the narrative, these characters endure and their stories lay foundations for hope in the future.

Every book is a collaborative effort and there a few people who I should single out for mention here.

Sue Gough was my mentor through the very initial stages of this project and she was instrumental in helping me navigate the complex emotional ground I wanted to draw out from my writing. Working with Sue fast forwarded my development as a writer and I'm pretty sure I wouldn't be who I am today without that formative experience. I would say more, but she also taught me the importance of brevity.

Carmel Bird saw something in an early draft of 'Frangipani' and encouraged me to rework and rewrite it. Through the process I grew to appreciate the marked differences between a story within a larger context and a story that has to stand alone as its own complete world.

Lisa Dempster has long championed my work and I still take it as a point of pride that she chose to publish 'Coda' as the first in a series of stories as stand-alone miniature volumes. It's entirely possible my fascination in messing around with form starts right there in her innovative work with Vignette and I take great satisfaction in bringing 'Coda' full circle, publishing it again in its own miniature volume for the boxed edition of this book.

Sue Wright is a sharp editor, a creative collaborator, and a publisher of singular taste and style. She has never once flinched when I have approached her with some harebrained idea. She also knows some of the city's best watering holes. I count myself lucky that I have a publisher prepared to get outraged on my behalf.

My favourite part of book making is the editorial stage and I had so much fun working with Stacey Clair to refine the stories and make them work collectively that I was kind of disappointed when we finished.

A text can only communicate well when it is combined with excellent design and, for *Ephemeral City*, those duties are split between Julia Favaloro and Alissa Dinallo. Julia's cover design and work on the ephemera are the result of a long, iterative process combined with an excellent eye for colour and balance. Alissa picked up from there and provided a wonderfully compatible internal design (she always knows how to make my words look classy). We also set the book in Doves Type, an early twentieth century typeface with a wild backstory of betrayal and petulance. Seriously, look it up.

Darren and Sean have read various versions of these stories through the years with comments, ideas, and the occasional beer. Jo has provided foundational and consistent support with a sympathetic ear and an encouraging word always at exactly the moment such things are needed. I can scarcely believe Xavier and Genevieve didn't exist when I recorded the first drafts of some of these stories. I'd like to think in the intervening years I have bestowed on them a deep appreciation for weird books. At the very least, they get a kick out of me giving them a shout in the acknowledgements.

Everyone else, you know who you are. Thanks.

Some sources
for the ephemera

'Smooth & Quiet' (Holden Advertisement),
>   *The Bulletin*, Vol. 86 No. 4390 (11 Apr 1964) p.72

Negative: Laurie Richards, Holden Car Display, International Motor Show,
>   Exhibition Buildings, c. 1963; Carlton, Victoria
>   Museums Victoria Collections
>   https://collections.museumsvictoria.com.au/items/801791

Art Union Ticket drawing No. 477, winning ticket No. 66027, Brisbane, 1937
>   Queensland Museum
>   https://collections.qm.qld.gov.au/objects/SH33710/golden-casket-art-union-ticket

Witnesses in a stabbing incident in Fortitude Valley, Brisbane, 1942
>   Digitised copy print from 28118 *Sunday Truth and Sunday Sun* Newspaper
>   Photographic Negatives
>   John Oxley Library, State Library of Queensland
>   https://onesearch.slq.qld.gov.au/permalink/61SLQ_INST/tqqf2h/
>   alma9918350513250206l

Trocadero dance topics, Brisbane, 1930
>   Brisbane Printers, Ltd.; Began with No. 1 (22 July, 1930)
>   State Library of Queensland
>   https://onesearch.slq.qld.gov.au/permalink/61SLQ_INST/tqqf2h/
>   alma9915053144702061

View looking down Jacob's Ladder towards Edward Street in Brisbane ca. 1940
>   John Oxley Library, State Library of Queensland
>   https://onesearch.slq.qld.gov.au/permalink/61SLQ_INST/3vt1h/
>   alma991838001392020611

Wilfred Owen, 'Disabled', 1917
>   https://www.bl.uk/collection-items/the-poetry-manuscripts-of-wilfred-owen
>   Owen's original manuscripts have been digitised at the British Library and are
>   worth your perusal.

W. B. Yeats, 'Byzantium', 1930
>   First published in *Words For Music Perhaps and Other Poems*, 1932

About the author

Simon Groth is a writer and long-time observer of publishing, technology, and the arts. His books include collections of rock music interviews, remixed short stories from the nineteenth century, and a novel whose order of chapters is randomised between copies.

With if:book Australia, Simon created a series of award-winning experimental works including the 24-Hour Book, live writing events at writers festivals around the world, and a city-wide challenge to write stories for digital billboards. His reporting on digital publishing has seen him travel the globe to discuss and explore the challenges and opportunities for writers and readers in a hyperconnected world.

marginalia

Between 2011 and 2016, I contributed a regular column to Writing Queensland magazine that ruminated on my work in progress and the state of technology and publishing at that time.

Since then, things have changed. Now is a strange and exciting time to think about how the written word fits into our lives. While the anxiety and optimism that surrounded 'the future of the book' has abated, the relationship between publishing and technology has only become more fascinating as the stakes have risen exponentially.

I think of marginalia as the successor to that column, short pieces on ideas big and small in a format that never takes itself too seriously.

Ex Libris

The metropole is a world of data-driven design and addled market saturation. It's a place where every decision, every movement is tracked and interpreted by the network to curate content for the comfort and containment of its citizens, where imagination and fiction are suppressed, and where books have been abandoned in favour of instant gratification.

Against this backdrop, a loose gathering of subversives collects the scraps of texts left behind. Calling themselves free readers, they seek to reconstruct a library from fragments away from the watchful eye of the feared committee for public safety. But what begins as the story of four people drawn to a band of literary misfits becomes an epic quest for truth in a world of lies and a narrative conscious of its own fictions.

Twelve of the chapters in this book are arranged at random, with each new copy shuffled anew, one of 479,001,600 possible variations. No two copies of *Ex Libris* are identical, and yet all tell the same story.